The ground was still mushy-soft, which was the reason Annabelle did not hear Luke approach. She jumped when she felt his hand touch her shoulder.

"Sorry, I didn't mean to frighten you."

Annabelle relaxed. "I didn't hear you come." She looked back at the children playing. "They are so happy to be outside again. Look how free they are."

"Thank you."

"For what?"

"For all your help, your work. You pitched in and did the work of two during this disaster."

"I couldn't do enough."

"I know. I felt that way too. Especially when Clara's parents were killed. If only I had gotten there sooner." He spoke of the little girl he had brought to Annabelle the night of the flood.

"But you saved her life!" Luke warmed under the encouragement of Annabelle, always so vibrant and spunky. He remembered how it used to get her into trouble and was pleased that she had learned to channel all that energy into helping others.

Wanting to express his affirmation, Luke reached out and placed his hands upon her shoulders. "Annabelle, the Lord's done a mighty work in you. You have become quite a woman."

The praise embarrassed Annabelle and she dropped her eyes momentarily and blushed. His kiss, then, came unexpectedly, and it was so gentle that she wondered if she had imagined it.

DIANNE L. CHRISTNER writes as "a means of expressing things on my heart." Dianne makes her home in Arizona with her husband and two children. *Lofty Ambitions* is the sequel to Dianne's **Heartsong Presents** debut, *Proper Intentions.*

Books by Dianne L. Christner

HEARTSONG PRESENTS
HP80—Proper Intentions

Lofty
Ambitions

Dianne L. Christner

A sequel to *Proper Intentions*

Heartsong Presents

With love to my mother,
Annabelle.

A note from the Author:
I love to hear from my readers! You may write to me at the
following address:

Dianne L. Christner
Author Relations
P.O. Box 719
Uhrichsville, OH 44683

ISBN 1-55748-634-4

LOFTY AMBITIONS

one

Annabelle's words slapped him, as hard as any physical blow might. He leaned against the rough timbers of Sheriff Buck Larson's jailhouse office to steady his trembling nerves. Then came the knockout punch. "As far as I'm concerned, this never happened," she snapped.

He had waited too long to give up easily, and moved toward her with outstretched arms. "Annabelle, please, hear me out."

"No! I won't listen to any more of this! When I walk out that door, Thaddeas, we shall end this nonsense. I hope you come to your senses!" The warning spewed forth with a fire that matched the woman's flame-colored hair.

Then she reeled about and marched defiantly to the massive wooden door. Though she strained, the door, warped and heavy, refused to budge. As Thaddeas watched her, his hopes—four years of patient waiting—dissolved like a puff of smoke before his eyes.

Annabelle pulled and tugged impatiently, but the door simply would not comply. She whirled to face Thaddeas, her green eyes ablaze with frustration. "Well?" Her bottom lip quivered and she tapped her high-heeled boot impatiently.

Like a man with a dagger in his heart, he moved to assist her. His dark face flinched and his arm tightened like a vise as he shouldered the door, which creaked open and stood ajar. Towering over her, though he was not tall as men go, he searched her face for some explanation. However, she bid him good day and flounced out the door.

Too distraught to cross the short distance to his adjoining room, Thaddeas collapsed in a heap in his uncle's chair. He leaned over the desk and ran his fingers through his thick, sable hair. A knot protruding in the grainy wood hypnotized him as he cross-examined himself. The questions he asked were painful, but necessary. *Had she misunderstood? Was she appalled by the idea?*

He'd never expected such a refusal. Disappointment flooded over him like a pool of black tar, thick and smothering, choking out his joy, his hopes, his dreams. His face buried in his hands, he did the only thing he knew. He prayed. "Oh Lord, what am I to do?"

Meanwhile, Annabelle marched toward her home in a huff. *Marry him, indeed!* A small stone lay in her path and she gave it a sound kick, rousing a wisp of dust. She continued at a brisk clip, muttering under her breath.

At seventeen, Annabelle Larson was a striking woman with an abundance of chestnut-colored hair and emerald eyes, but she was also headstrong and spoiled. If blame could be placed, life's circumstances ranked high.

Orphaned at the age of one at the Big Bottom Indian massacre of 1791, Annabelle and her two sisters grew up in Beaver Creek, Ohio, under the overly protective care of Mattie Tucker. Their home, referred to as Tucker House by the townspeople, was living quarters and Mattie's seamstress shop combined.

During Annabelle's impressionable adolescent years, a tragic wagon accident nearly claimed her life. A long recovery set the scene, and Annabelle was unduly pampered by her family and friends. A short time later, Mattie's marriage to Sheriff Buck Larson accentuated the problem. Blinded by his long-standing love for Mattie, he also spoiled his wife's adopted daughters.

This had little effect on Annabelle's married sister, Kate. Claire, Annabelle's younger sister, also remained unscathed. Any indulgence lavished on the latter only blossomed into a flower of kindness, which she in turn bestowed upon others.

Her sympathy for people vexed Annabelle, who was impatient and impetuous. The two sisters were as different as night and day—angel and vixen.

As Annabelle neared her home, a groan escaped her pursed lips when Claire appeared, coming from the direction of the hen house. A sensitive creature of sixteen, Claire saw the world through a pair of blue eyes set in a peaches-and-cream face of rather plain features. Straw-colored hair fluttered loose across her back and face as she strolled toward Annabelle with a basket of eggs in the crook of her arm. Claire brightened when she saw her sister. "Annabelle, wait!"

"Oh, Claire, not now. Please, not now." Annabelle brushed her aside and hurried into the house, only to encounter a second member of her family.

"Oh, hello, Annabelle. Is Buck comin' shortly?" Mattie paused from stirring a kettle of beans long enough to wipe her hands on the apron wrapped about her straight, slim figure.

"I-I didn't see him," Annabelle stammered as she rushed by and mounted the steps, two at a time, leading to her room. Alone at last, she slammed the door and heaved herself onto the bed. A gamut of emotions teamed together and surged forth in a torrent of tears. When the storm eventually subsided, she was left feeling drained.

Like a wilted lettuce leaf, she lay draped across her bed while the scene in Buck's office easily coaxed itself into the forefront of her mind's stage. Her excuses came to play.

She could not marry a cousin! This was rationalization at its best for Thaddeas was not a blood relative. Sheriff Buck Larson adopted Annabelle and Claire when he married Mattie Tucker, giving them his name. Therefore, even though Thaddeas was Buck's nephew, the three young people were not blood related. This fact, however, escaped Annabelle at the moment.

Thaddeas loved the West, but she wanted to go east. With a shudder she thought of her older sister, Kate, toiling on the

Potter farm. Annabelle wanted more than that. If she married, he would have to be rich so she could live like Dorie.

Her friend Dorie, whose father owned the general store in Beaver Creek, had moved away to attend school in Cincinnati. Then, after graduating, she moved to Charleston to live with relatives, where she now frequented balls, and handsome men attended her every whim and desire. Annabelle waited greedily for her letters to arrive, which read like novels—or fairy tales—and whet Annabelle's appetite for the flamboyant lifestyle.

Leaning over the side of her bed, Annabelle groped a moment and pulled out a small wooden chest, disturbing a nest of dust bunnies. Opening the lid with trembling fingers, she unfolded the last letter from her lifelong friend and read:

> *I do not believe I shall ever return to Beaver Creek except to visit. After being introduced to society, it would be hard to return to a life of wearing calico and waiting upon customers. My mama gave up a great deal when she allowed Papa to pursue his dreams of the West. I hope you shall not hold it against me or think I am uppity.*

Annabelle sighed and envisioned a magnificent ballroom filled with gallant gentlemen who danced with beautiful ladies. Fantasizing, she saw herself floating in the arms of a handsome cavalier. She fluttered her eyelashes and stole a glance at his face. To her horror, it portrayed her cousin's image.

She shivered as she recalled the hurt look on Thad's face and sat up shakily, dabbing at her eyes. What a predicament! She needed to talk to Kate. Her head throbbed and burned like fever. Copper ringlets clung tenaciously to her damp brow, and she moved toward the basin of water on her stand to splash her face. Annabelle paled. What if Thaddeas told the sheriff? How could she face Buck at supper?

Her fears materialized. Sheriff Larson stopped in to close up his office and found Thaddeas bent over the desk. "Thaddeas?"

"Oh, Uncle Buck. Is it that late already? I hadn't noticed," Thaddeas mumbled.

"Thaddeas, Son. Is something wrong?" Concern showed in every movement of the sheriff's massive body.

"I'm just feeling low, Uncle Buck."

"You want to tell me about it?" The sheriff prodded his nephew gently.

"I-I offered for Annabelle. I asked her to marry me." In embarrassment, Thaddeas fixed his eyes on his boots, polished to a shine, and then stared at the floor.

"Yeah? What did she say?"

"She was angry, didn't want anything to do with me. She said she'd just pretend I never said anything, then she left." Thaddeas moaned. "Uncle Buck, all these years, I've loved her. I've waited so long for her to grow up and now she refused me. I don't know what I'll do."

"Give her time to think on it, Thad. She's a high-strung filly. You know that. If you're patient, she might come around."

"It's hard to figure a woman's mind."

"I know she cares for you." The sheriff patted his nephew's arm, not knowing what else to say, and waited until Thaddeas finally roused.

"Uncle Buck, you better head home or Mattie will worry about you. I'm going to my room and get some rest now. I've got a big day tomorrow at the mill. David Green purchased a huge order of timber and all the journals have to be entered right away for he has a buyer coming from Cincinnati."

"All right then, but don't fret, Thad. You know God is big enough for this. He knows what's best for you, and how you're hurting."

"I know, Uncle Buck." The sheriff watched Thaddeas shuffle across the room and enter his lodging without a backward look. Buck headed home. The memory of Thad's droopy shoulders plagued him, but he remained at an impasse. What could he do?

That evening at supper, Annabelle suspected that Buck knew about Thad's proposal because of his reflective mood. Afraid that his eyes would undress her soul, she refused to look up and pushed her food around her plate with her fork. Then a muffled cough and the clearing of Buck's throat as if he were about to speak broke the silence. She clenched her fists beneath the table and waited for a rebuke, but he did not utter a sound. Although Buck longed to intervene, in his wisdom gathered from years of serving folks, he did not.

&

Much later the same evening, wrapped in darkness and tucked in quiet, Annabelle gave way to tears—not overwrought, but calm as a summer shower, relinquishing stress and stubbornness. As she lay still, her thoughts raced, searching for a remedy. Ah yes, she would see Kate on Sunday! They were invited for the noonday meal. She felt better already. Surely Kate could help. Then her heart skipped a beat. Thaddeas! He would be there also.

two

Annabelle looked around the familiar schoolroom where she had spent her school days and where folks still gathered for their Sunday meetings. A movement across the room caught her eye, and she watched as Melanie Caldwell, formerly Whitfield, stretched her right hand across her left shoulder to tug at her shawl. It slipped and hung in soft ripples like a snowdrift about her back.

Then a long, thin arm reached out, grasped the shawl, and placed it lovingly back onto her shoulders, resting there a moment in an affectionate gesture before moving away. In her left arm Melanie held a newborn, her second, a dumpling of a little girl. A pudgy, red-faced toddler sat on his father's knee.

Annabelle smiled as she recalled how Melanie had chased after her sister Kate's husband, Ben Wheeler, before they were married. It had piqued Melanie when Ben wed Kate, but then Charlie Caldwell had moved into Beaver Creek and Melanie married him soon after.

This reminded her of Thaddeas' proposal. Blushing, she straightened and strained to hear Reverend Wheeler's sermon.

"'Reckless words pierce like a sword, but the tongue of the wise brings healing,' Proverbs 12:18 says." The reverend continued, "'He who guards his lips guards his soul, but he who speaks rashly will come to ruin.'" The preacher looked around the room. "That's found in Proverbs 13:3. Folks, remember this week to treat each other with care. Let us pray." Annabelle shivered. The preacher's words settled and lay in the pit of her stomach like hard pebbles.

On the dirt road that led from the schoolhouse to the old

Potter place where Kate and Ben now lived, there was much to attract Annabelle's attention. In September the air was fresh and the leaves were blushing, turning, and curling under the caress of the night's cold air, but Annabelle was oblivious to autumn's crisp call.

Her attention focused on the backside of Thaddeas Larson. His torso slightly bent, he rode ahead, but far enough behind Kate and Ben to avoid their dust. Thad had not spoken to her today, and she missed his friendly bantering, yet at the same time dreaded his company. She sighed and tried to tear her eyes away from the creaking leather of his saddle and concentrate on her sister's wagon, leading the procession.

Up ahead, Ben consoled his wife. "I know it hurts when Melanie says those things, but don't let it get you down, Kate. I'd like a baby, too, but we have each other, don't we?" His blue eyes glistened with emotion.

"You're right, Ben. I suppose the Lord knew it was all I could do just to handle you," she teased. Then growing serious, "Pa's right though, reckless words do 'pierce like a sword'." Kate used the name "Pa" fondly, since her own folks died in an Indian raid when she was six. Now Emmett Wheeler was her father-in-law.

Her husband replied, "Melanie's always had trouble with her tongue. Pa also said, 'he who speaks rashly will come to ruin.' We must be kind, because she's sure to bring trouble upon herself."

"Her baby is lovely. My arms ache for a child, Ben."

"I know, Kate. I know," he whispered.

Peeking just around the fringe of forest on their left was the "old Potter place." It was not really old. Mary Potter had once lived there with her first husband and two sons, James and Frank. When the Wheelers moved into Beaver Creek, she was widowed. Later she married Emmett Wheeler, and folks started referring to it as the "old Potter place." Even after Ben and

Kate moved in, the name seemed to stick, as there was already a Wheeler farm and old habits are hard to break.

It spread out before them now, a cabin, barn, corrals, and a large amount of land where field corn had earlier waved brown-tasseled heads. The spread was well cared for, as Ben loved farming. He once told Kate it came as natural to him as breathing. The land responded favorably to each loving and weary touch from its master.

The wagons pulled into the lane and rolled to a stop. Everyone was hungry, anticipating Sunday dinner, and scattered to help prepare the meal or do the necessary outdoor chores. Time passed quickly and soon their stomachs were full, yet they lingered around the table.

Sheriff Larson put out the bait, "I got a copy of the *Western Star* in the wagon."

"The *Western Star*?" questioned Ben. "What's that, Buck?"

"It's the newspaper out of Lebanon, brand new," the sheriff explained.

"How did you get it, Uncle?" Thaddeas asked.

"Well now, remember that fellow by the name of Stone that I locked up yesterday for disturbing the peace?" Thaddeas nodded and the sheriff continued. "He had it on him and, of course, I procured all his belongings before I locked him up. Anyway, when he left he said to keep it, not that he was overly friendly or anything. Believe me, he wasn't!" The sheriff chuckled and Ben grinned.

"Anything in there about the Burr trial?" asked Thaddeas, lifting his dark eyebrows in interest. Raised in Boston, Thaddeas had rubbed shoulders with men of the world in his father's leather shop. This influence instilled at an early age a fascination for the country's politics.

"Yes, Son, as a matter of fact, there is."

Annabelle looked across the table and wondered what this trial could be about. It was the first thing that had perked

Thaddeas up all day. She searched his eyes for their familiar sparkle—they normally brimmed with life—when they suddenly blinked and stared back at her. She blushed and looked away. A glimmer of light shone until they had met hers, then they turned to dark pools.

Later, when Kate moved to clear the table, the women rose to help while the men sauntered into the sitting room, and Sheriff Larson went out to the wagon for his *Western Star.* After much discussion about the notorious Aaron Burr, tried for treason and accused of enticing young men to follow him as the head of a revolutionary party, Thaddeas left to stretch his legs.

When he opened the door that led outside, he stopped in his tracks. Annabelle sat on the step, her back to him, perched like a red squirrel on a stump. He breathed a prayer, swallowed for courage, and moved to join her. As he settled on the step beside her he sensed her stiffening body, but she turned and acknowledged him. "Thaddeas."

"Annabelle," he said in a soft tone, "I want to apologize for . . ."

Annabelle interrupted him before he could finish his sentence. "Thaddeas, I told you it never happened! Now, I don't want to hear another word about it."

Thaddeas protested, "It did happen, and I am sorry that I offended you. I was wrong. I thought you cared about me."

"I do care about you, silly, we're cousins. I just don't want to spoil our friendship. You're like a brother to me, Thad."

"Like a brother?"

"That's right. And another thing, you love it here."

"Pardon?"

"The wild West . . . Beaver Creek." She waved her arms to refer to the countryside. "I want to live in the city, see new places, dress in fine gowns, wear jewels, and attend balls like Dorie."

"I see." Her shallow response disappointed Thad. "I've lived in the city, Annabelle. Not everyone goes to balls, only the wealthy. There is also poverty and filth." He studied her reaction.

Without batting an eye she challenged him, "And what is wrong with wealth? Sure isn't any around this place."

Thaddeas brooded over her words. She was still a child. Oh, why did he have to be in love with her? When Thaddeas did not respond, she grew uneasy. To change the subject, she flashed him a brilliant smile and coaxed with her eyes. "Stop moping! Let's do something. It's boring just sitting here . . ." Her voice broke off when she saw something that gave her a fright. "Thad," she whispered, "there is someone watching us, over there in that clump of trees past the barn." She did not point, but nodded her head in the direction of the barn.

"Stay here!" Thaddeas jumped to his feet in one swift movement and sped toward the spot Annabelle had indicated. "Halt!" He yelled as he ran, but the dark figure also ran, and quickly disappeared into the wooded area in the direction of Beaver Creek. Thaddeas raced until he was out of breath then stopped, panting, and leaned against a tree. The man was nowhere to be found. Thad moved in a wide circle, retracing his steps back to the place where they had seen him lurking in the shadows.

Annabelle soon joined him, her skirt flying. "Did you see him?"

Thaddeas ignored her question and searched the ground for clues, touching the deep tracks where the trespasser had stood. They looked at each other. It had not been their imaginations. "Thad! Was it an Indian?"

"No."

"What do you think he wanted?"

"I don't know. But I'm sure it's nothing to worry about. I'd better mention it to Ben, though." His forehead furrowed in concern. He knew that Ben was a peace-loving man who avoided confrontations, but he felt Ben would want to know.

The sudden fright and brisk run invigorated Thad and he suddenly felt better. He gave Annabelle a broad grin. "And you were bored. Come on, let's go tell the others." Relieved that he seemed his old self again, she slipped her arm through his.

Later, when Thad led the men out to look at the prowler's tracks, Annabelle saw her chance to speak with Kate. She grabbed her sister's arm and whispered, "Could we talk?" Soon they were sitting across from one another sipping cups of strong coffee.

"Now, Annabelle, what seems to be the problem? Do you know the trespasser?"

"No, of course not. It has nothing to do with that. I just thought we might have a moment alone." Annabelle realized she did not have much time until the rest would return. She squirmed on the wooden bench, then jumped right in. "Thad asked me to marry him."

"What? How wonderful, Annabelle!"

"No! It is not wonderful!" she retorted. "I don't want to marry him. His notions are going to spoil a perfectly fine friendship that we have enjoyed for many years."

"You are a beautiful young woman. You cannot expect for your relationships with men to stay the same. It is only natural that some will be attracted to you. Don't you care for Thaddeas?"

"Of course I do. But not that way."

"Perhaps then," Kate considered, "Thaddeas isn't right for you. However, I've known for a long time that he loved you, Annabelle. You must realize that things probably will never be the same between you again. Either his love will draw you to him or drive you away. He's a fine young man. Take time to think it through, and don't do anything rash that you'll be sorry for later." Kate patted Annabelle's hand. "Now I'm done lecturing you."

"Nothing troubles you, does it, Kate?"

"What do you mean?"

"You work hard and take whatever comes your way without complaining. How can you be content on the farm, working from sunrise to sunset? I want more out of life."

"So do I," Kate whispered. "I want a baby." A large tear rolled like a crystal jewel down her white velvet cheek.

"I-I'm so sorry," Annabelle stammered. "I didn't know."

"Well," Kate said dabbing at her cheek, "now you do. But, back to your problem, Annabelle. You said that farm life was not what you wanted, but that is not what Thaddeas wants either, is it?"

"Well, I guess not . . ." She cut her answer short as the others entered discussing the prowler.

"I wouldn't worry about it, Ben," the sheriff was saying. "Probably just a passerby."

"Strange, though," Ben mumbled, as he scratched his chin with his huge brown hand.

three

The giant saw, powered from the Little Miami River, turned the great wheels that gave life to the mill and the men that worked there. The tool's buzzing intensified to a high-pitched roar and then suddenly returned to the whining hum, typical of the usual background drone with which Thaddeas did his work. This meant someone had opened the door to the outer room and closed it again. Thad wondered if it was David Green, coming after the bill of sale that he was figuring. He quickly finished multiplying the numbers before him.

Then he heard the door to his cubbyhole office creak and glanced up to see Sheriff Larson's huge physique standing in the doorway. "Oh, it's you, Uncle Buck. Come in and have a seat, and I'll be with you in just a minute."

The sheriff nodded and settled into a chair across the desk from Thaddeas and watched with pride. Buck had never had a son of his own, and it pleased him to treat his nephew—who had braved the West to seek him out—as one.

"What can I do for you, Uncle Buck?" Thaddeas pushed aside his bill of sale.

"I just came from Cooper's General Store, and they had this letter from your folks. Thought I'd deliver it."

Thaddeas reached for the letter and leaned back in his chair, tilting it onto two legs as he tore open the envelope. He was always glad to get news from home, and Buck was eager to hear from his brother as well. He smoothed the letter out and began to read.

Dearest Thad,
I am filled with sorrow. Your father, my beloved

*husband, died this past night. He took ill, developing
lung fever.*

Thaddeas' chair slammed to the floor and his eyes filled
with tears, which he brushed away with the back of his hand.
His fingers trembled as he tried to read further, but his vision
blurred.

"Son? What is it?" The sheriff instantly rose to his feet and
went around the desk toward Thaddeas.

"It's Father. He died." Thaddeas looked up at Buck through
pain-filled, unbelieving eyes. "Father's dead," he repeated.

"Lewis? Lewis is dead?" the sheriff asked. He pulled a stool
to Thaddeas' side and slumped down onto it with his thick
legs and gun-belted middle spilling over. His hand gripped his
nephew's shoulder. "I'm so sorry, Son." After a moment he
asked, "Is there more?"

"Yes, here. I-I can't see the words." The sheriff gently took
the piece of paper and read aloud.

*He has been abed this past week. I should have writ-
ten earlier to tell you of his illness, but I was holding on
to every thread of hope that he would not leave this world
behind. He spoke of many things before he parted, expressing his love for you, his youngest son. I know that
he envied your adventure, going west and all, wishing it
could have been him. Your brother, Leon, is keeping
things going at the shop, but he wants you to come home
at once so the will can be read. I know that you love the
West, Son, but we sorely need you. Please come as speedi-
ly as you can. My heart breaks for the loss of your father
and the grief that this letter brings to you.*

*Love,
Mother*

Please give my regrets to Buck.

Thaddeas bent over the desk and placed his head in his hands, his shoulders shaking. Buck embraced him, and they both let the tears run freely as the realization of death sank in.

After a long time passed, the sheriff spoke with compassion in his voice. "Stay put and I'll find David Green." Minutes later Buck returned for Thaddeas. They moved past towering stacks of clapboards and floorboards. The sweet smell of wood and sawdust went unnoticed as they walked on, heavy footed, past stockpiles of shingles, staves, and rails. Finally they turned west—with their backs toward the river and the giant wheels that splashed and groaned an appropriate requiem—and walked silently toward the jailhouse.

❧

By the following evening, things were in order and Thaddeas rode to Tucker House to say good-bye. The mill's owner, David Green, did not want to let his employee go, but he paid him what he had coming. He offered his regrets and promised to take Thaddeas back if he should return to Ohio. Mr. Green saw potential in Thaddeas, acknowledging him as an agreeable young man who had done a remarkable job with the mill's accounts. He would miss him.

Mattie convinced the sheriff that she would be fine if he accompanied Thaddeas on the first leg of his journey. She knew rumors of Indian unrest along the Miami and Ohio Rivers worried Buck. At first the sheriff hesitated, but then he quickly made plans. He rode out to Jude Miller's place and persuaded him to watch over the town for a week or so in his absence, deputizing him and giving him a long list of instructions. Then he set about buying the staples they would need for their trip. Finishing up with some last-minute details at his office, he picked Thaddeas up there and started toward Tucker House.

Mattie greeted them as they tethered their horses. "Buck! Thaddeas!" Linking her arms in each of theirs, she led them to the house. When they reached the steps, she turned to Thaddeas and said, "It hurts me, Thaddeas, to see ya suffer. I'm so sorry for ya."

"I know, Mattie. Thank you."

During supper, Claire could hardly eat. She swallowed hard and blinked back tears, brokenhearted to see Thaddeas go through such a hard time. Thaddeas cleared his throat, and she gave her full attention. "I've done a lot of thinking today. You're my family, and I love Ohio. I don't want to leave, but Boston is my duty. I don't know if I'll be back. I'll miss you all."

Mattie spoke quietly, "Sometimes life's portions are hard ta take, sure enough, Thaddeas. But you're a man of God and I know you'll be strong. You'll make it through. We are family, Thad. And we're gonna miss ya somethin' fierce."

"Thank you for letting Uncle Buck see me off. But he doesn't have to come, you know."

"He needs ta go. It's important to him," Mattie replied. The sheriff smiled across the table at the woman he loved.

After dinner Thaddeas approached Annabelle. "I need to talk with you a minute, please, before I leave." It had been a shock when Thaddeas had asked her to marry him, and now it was a greater blow that he was departing from her life altogether. She thought her heart would break to lose him, but upon seeing his sorrow, she answered calmly, "All right, Thad."

He led her to the wooden bench beneath the giant hickory tree beside the house. As Annabelle sat down she took great pains to arrange her skirt about her. It was something to do. Thaddeas sat close at her side. "Oh, Thaddeas!" she blurted out, "I'm so sorry."

"I-I never thought it would come to this," he said softly. Annabelle looked up, her eyes brimming with unshed tears, and he continued—straight to the point, "I love you, Annabelle."

"I love you too, Thaddeas."

His eyes brightened at her words and his eyebrows raised to ask the unspoken question that stuck in his throat. He urged, "Marry me, then."

Annabelle remembered Kate's words. *His love will either draw you closer or drive you further apart. Don't say anything that you will be sorry for later.* She brushed away a tear that escaped her thick lashes, then reached out to take his hand. He felt the wetness as she answered. "Thaddeas, I can't. My heart is breaking, but I cannot marry you."

He applied pressure to his grip on her hand and asked. "You don't love me then?"

"Not in that way, Thad. But I don't want to lose you. What will I do without you?"

"I don't know if I'll be back."

"You must come back," she pleaded.

"Why? If I cannot have you, Annabelle, I'd be better off to stay in Boston."

"But you love the West. You said the city was too crowded, that . . ."

"Maybe I'll go somewhere else, farther west across the Mississippi. I feel dead inside, Annabelle."

"I do, too," she answered.

"We'd better head back to the house. I need to get home. We'll be leaving early in the morning." Then he turned and said almost desperately, "Annabelle, if you ever change your mind, I'll be there."

Annabelle felt like nothing would ever be right in her world again.

four

The flatboat glided smoothly downstream, riding the current of the Little Miami like a leaf catching hold of the skirts of the wind, yet not so free. David Lowry's able hands maneuvered the raft around rocks, trees, and the other obstacles that threatened their voyage.

Thaddeas sat near the edge, hugging his knees and scanning the shoreline. The trees passed like great dark giants, sentinels of a forbidden land. Cynical thoughts nagged at him. *Banished! Snatched from the wilderness that I love.* He reached up to brush away a tear lest his uncle see him cry, then expelled a weary sigh along with a sidelong glance in Buck's direction.

Buck hoped to direct his nephew's attention away from his troubles. "That's all military-occupied land." The sheriff pointed to the east side of the shore where Thad had been staring. "It's the Virginia Military Reserve."

This part of the country was new to him. Thaddeas nodded. Then Buck pointed to round hills that looked like burial sites, and the young man's thoughts returned to the death of his father. "See those mounds, Son? It makes a body wonder what sort of people made them."

Thaddeas choked out the words, "Indians, I suppose."

"Too bad you folks ain't goin' down river further," Lowry piped up. "You're gonna miss the great wall."

"Great wall?" Thaddeas looked at the man in wonder.

"That's right," the navigator replied. "Three and a half miles long."

"Have you seen it, Uncle Buck?"

23

"Yep. It's a sight, made out of earth, stone, and bone."

"Never get tired of seein' it," Lowry remarked, as he deftly steered the boat from the back with a long oar. "Looks like an old snake crawlin' in the grass alongside the Miami."

"Is it a fort?" Thaddeas asked.

"I reckon. No one knows for sure. Folks say it encloses one hundred acres of those mounds." Lowry nodded his woolly head. His words muffled as he leaned over the back of the barge and spit out a mouthful of black juice. Then he continued. "See that knob just ahead? I'm steerin' towards it. When we pass the point, you'll be able to see Waynesville, where you'll be goin' ashore." He grunted and with powerful strokes guided the barge toward the landmark.

True to the man's word, the settlement soon appeared. In minutes Lowry had docked the boat, helped Buck and Thaddeas get their horses ashore, and pushed off again towards his final destination of New Orleans. The horses were skittish and the two men spoke soothing words before they mounted. Then they wasted no time leaving the small settlement in their dust, traveling toward Cincinnati by means of the Waynesville road.

☙

Stiff from hours in the saddle, Thaddeas arched his back and stretched his arms. They had ridden hard all afternoon except for stopping twice to rest the horses and drink water, and once when they had lunched alongside the trail. The beautiful spot with a trickling stream had reminded Thaddeas of the many times he had fished behind Tucker House with the girl he left behind. Now there were only dense forests for as far as the eye could see.

"Are you as tuckered out as I am, Son?" asked the sheriff as he rode alongside Thaddeas.

"I feel rusty as an old tin can," Thad replied.

"Well, we'll be hitting Lebanon and the Golden Lamb in a couple hours."

"I think any place would look good tonight," Thaddeas sighed. Fatigue creased his face with heavy strokes and sorrow shadowed his eyes.

"The first couple days of travel are always the worst," Buck said solemnly. He thought about the long trail ahead for his nephew and the ordeal that awaited him when he reached Boston.

As the first shades of night fell, they pulled up weary but grateful at the hitching post of the Golden Lamb. "A welcome sight, and just in time. I think the cold weather is heading in." Buck pointed toward the inn. Thaddeas nodded, taking in the two-story log tavern where a wooden sign, displaying the Golden Lamb emblem, creaked and groaned in the nippy night air.

A lad ran to greet them. "If yar stayin' at the inn, I'll take yar horses for ya."

"That we are. Thank you," Buck said. "We'll check in on them before we turn in. Is supper still being served?"

"Yes, sir. Veal, cheese, cornbread, and pie, sir."

"Sounds tempting. Come on, Thad."

Once inside, a full-fleshed woman warmly greeted them. She led them to their room so they could clean up, and said, "My name's Martha. Jest seat yourselves at the table in the dinin' room when yar ready, and I'll serve ya yar meal." She bustled away and the clacking sound of her heels echoed in the narrow hallway. Buck spotted a basin of water, and they quickly washed for supper.

"We best eat so we can turn in," Buck suggested.

"Hope it's as good as it smells." Thaddeas followed his uncle back through the hall and into a large dining area equipped with a huge table where folks sat before the meal the stable boy had described. Buck nodded with approval. He knew the place; it looked good as ever. A cloth graced the table, and a hearth fire warmed the room.

A stern-looking military man passed Buck a platter of ham and veal. He introduced himself politely, "Lieutenant Wade Brooks."

"Buck Larson, and this is my nephew, Thaddeas."

"I see you're a sheriff. Where you from?"

"Just upriver, Beaver Creek, but Thaddeas is a Bostonian. He's on his way home. And you, Lieutenant?"

"Stationed at Fort Wayne under the command of Captain William Wells at the moment, originally from Pittsburgh."

"Really? Same as my wife, Mattie."

"I didn't know that, Uncle Buck," Thaddeas interrupted. "I guess I never heard Mattie talk about her family."

Buck turned and directed his conversation toward his nephew. "Yep. She grew up in Pennsylvania. She isn't one to talk much of her past. It's painful for her. She didn't get on with her folks. Her father, the Reverend Tucker, was a strict, mulish man . . . ."

Brooks choked on his drink and Buck cut his explanation short. "You all right, Lieutenant?"

The tall rugged man looked quite pale. He nodded. "Yes, please excuse me."

Buck resumed his conversation with Thad. "It wasn't her fault, she's a good woman."

"Of course, Uncle Buck."

Buck stabbed a chunk of meat with his fork and daydreamed about his wife. He pictured her at work, stitching something pretty for one of her customers. Loneliness pricked his already heavy heart.

Thaddeas addressed the officer, "Lieutenant Brooks, what can you tell us about the Indian situation? Does the military expect trouble?"

"It doesn't look good. A settler by the name of Myer was killed, scalped a few miles west of Urbana. A lot of folks are packing off to Kentucky for safety." The hair on Thaddeas' neck bristled at the news and his eyes widened. "We're keeping a close watch on the Indian chief Tecumseh and his brother, the Prophet, up at Greenville. Have you heard any reports about that pair?"

Thad shook his head. "No, sir."

Buck joined in the conversation. "But we've noticed lots of Indians milling around lately."

"Actually I'm headed to talk to some Shakers about the Indian village of Greenville," the lieutenant explained. "They paid them a visit not too long ago."

"What does Captain Wells think about it all?" Buck asked.

"Tecumseh and the Prophet vow they want peace. However, at the same time, they are uniting tribes from all over the northwest territory, even across the Mississippi. Tribes you've never heard of. The captain thinks it looks mighty suspicious. I think the settlers in Ohio need to be on the lookout."

Buck pushed his plate away from him and sank back in his chair. He hated to hear that kind of talk. Things had been peaceful in Ohio for a long time, but the lieutenant was right. His heart sank with the heaviness that had plagued him over the last several days. It was late and he felt tired.

"Ready to turn in, Thad?"

Meanwhile, back at the old Potter place, Ben pulled the barn door closed. *Almost dark*, he thought. *I'm late for supper. Hope Kate's feathers aren't ruffled.* Then he remembered that Annabelle had spent the day with Kate. He pictured them engrossed in women talk and realized he need not worry. Approaching the house, he picked up his gait, anticipating the meal that would be waiting as well as the companionship of the young women inside. Their silhouettes in the window drew his attention, then he gasped as his eyes caught a figure squatted low, peering into the window where Kate and Annabelle could clearly be seen by the lantern light.

"What in the . . . Hey you!" Ben bolted toward the crouched man, who jumped when he realized he had been discovered. Instantly, the stranger made for the side of the house and slipped around the back with Ben close behind. "Wait! Hold up, now!" Ben yelled as he gained on the shadow, which enlarged with each step.

A thought skimmed his mind, one of relief that the prowler was not an Indian. Ben was almost within reach and was grabbing for the man's coat when his own foot caught in a tangle of roots and weeds, wrenching his lower leg and jerking him to a stop in midflight. His feet went out from under him and he sailed forward, hitting the ground with his head. He lay stunned, and several minutes passed before he groggily returned to consciousness. As he recovered, he groped about in the dark.

Ben tried to focus, but his head throbbed and he was overcome with dizziness. Blood oozed down his brow. He raised himself to a sitting position and remembered the trespasser. Everything was now dark, and he knew the stranger would be long gone, so he eased himself to his feet and limped toward the house. Before he could reach it, he heard his name ring out in the night air.

"Ben!" Kate's voice came from the barn where she had gone to search for him. Seeing the blood streaming down his face, she screamed, "Darling! What happened?" Instantly she supported her husband and guided him inside, easing him into a chair where she grabbed a clean towel and pressed it to the wound. Then she undid the top button of his shirt.

"Ben! Kate?" Annabelle rushed to their sides.

"I feel better. I'm fine now," Ben whispered.

"Please, stay put. We must be sure the bleeding stops, then I'll take another look," his wife ordered while glancing up at Annabelle.

She saw terror in Kate's eyes and knelt on the floor beside the pair, watching mutely. Annabelle grabbed Ben's sleeve and clung fiercely, while he gently scolded his attentive wife.

"Listen, Kate. You shouldn't have gone to the barn alone after dark. There could be animals, Indians, or prowlers."

"Don't be ridiculous." Kate's voice quivered, "I just went to look for you. I knew you were out there. Now, if you must talk, tell me what happened."

"I-I guess I tripped and hit my head on a rock or something. It must have knocked me out."

"All right. Let's take another look." Kate examined her husband's wound carefully. "It's not deep," she sighed with relief. Then she pressed the towel on the cut again. "Hold this, Darling, and just sit still. I'll get you a drink."

Annabelle quickly jumped up. "No, I'll get it, Kate." Ben watched his sister-in-law dip a cup of water with her back toward him, then he looked into Kate's moist and troubled eyes. The brown swallowed up the green flecks that usually danced there. She was on the verge of tears.

Ben did not like to keep anything from Kate, but did not want to frighten her, either. He would ride into town the next day to talk to Buck.

five

The wagon jostled Ben and Annabelle as its large-spoked wheels cranked along the road, frigid in the early morning cold. Annabelle clutched her cloak and glanced at her brother-in-law, who unconsciously tugged on his hat to cover the gash on his forehead. He refused to wear the outlandish bandage that Kate had tried to force upon him.

Annabelle shivered. "I cannot believe how cold it is this morning."

"Mm hm."

"The trees will soon be bare with this sudden drop in temperature."

"Mm hm."

Annabelle grinned when she realized Ben was not listening to a word she said. "I suppose I mentioned that I was eloping on Saturday?"

"Mm hm."

His mind rehearsed the previous night's episode, reliving the scene a hundred times. This morning he had awakened, remembering that Sheriff Larson had accompanied Thaddeas to Cincinnati. His head exploded with each toss of the wagon as he tried to recall who the sheriff had deputized and sort out what should be done.

"Ben Wheeler, you are the most preoccupied man I know." Annabelle leaned forward, positioning pink cheeks close to his so he could not escape her miffed expression.

"I'm sorry, Annabelle. I'm not very good company this morning. My head feels like it met the end of a tomahawk, but don't tell your sister."

"Oh, Ben, I didn't realize. I'm the one that should apologize."

Ben smiled warmly and patted her hand, "No need."

They rode the remaining distance to Tucker House in silence. Then Annabelle offered, "I can help myself down, Ben, unless you would like to come in?"

"Yes. I would like to chat with Mattie a bit."

Annabelle hurried into the house, leaving him to secure his rig. "Mattie! I'm home."

"Mornin', Annabelle. Did ya have a good visit?"

"Yes, very good. Ben wants to talk to you."

"Oh?" Mattie laid aside her sewing and found Ben waiting on the porch.

"Good morning, Mattie."

"Mornin'. Come on in," she invited.

"Ah, no. I just want to check if there is anything you need, with Buck gone."

"That's kind of ya, but no, I can't think of anythin'. Takin' Annabelle off my hands for a spell was plenty." Mattie winked at Ben, while mentally linking Annabelle's strange behavior of late to Thad's departure.

He chuckled. "I expect Kate got the brunt of that." Then his voice took on a serious but indifferent tone, for he did not want to worry Mattie. "By the way, who did the sheriff put in charge of the town?"

"Jude Miller."

"I see. Well, let me know if you hear from Buck or need a hand with anything."

"All right, thank ya," Mattie called as she watched Ben return to his wagon with a stiff gait. She wondered if he was overdoing it around the farm with heavy lifting. Then she turned her attention to Annabelle and hoped her visit with Kate had lifted her spirits. When she entered the sitting room and picked up her sewing, she found Claire conversing with her sister.

"I'm walking to town this morning to get some things that I need for my box."

"What box?"

"For the box social, Sunday night." Claire stole a glance at Annabelle, who slumped in her chair like a giant rag doll at the mere mention of the event.

"It just won't be the same without Thad," Annabelle whimpered.

"It will be fun." Claire coaxed her sister. Though she was the younger by a year and a half, Claire oftentimes acted the more mature. "Come with me. You always have such good ideas."

"Well, I don't know." Annabelle mumbled, "Mattie may need me. I was gone all day yesterday."

"Go along," Mattie waved her needle in the air. "But, when you get back, I'm puttin' ya both ta work."

Annabelle rose reluctantly to follow Claire out of the room. "Bundle up now, it's cold outside," Mattie warned in a voice garbled from a mouth stuffed with pins.

∂

As they fingered the slick, satin ribbons in Cooper's General Store, Annabelle admonished Claire, "Mattie's got plenty of lace at home, but a few sticks of candy would be nice." Her mind raced, and she imagined the young men she knew contesting over their boxed lunches.

Gradually her attitude changed to excitement, and she hastened toward the candy counter where the mild scents of cinnamon and mint mixed with the heavier aromas of coffee and molasses. A balding head poked around the corner of a row of glass jars filled with tempting confections. Elias Cooper straightened to his full height and beamed when he saw who his customers were.

"Mornin' Annabelle, Claire."

"Hello, Mr. Cooper."

Annabelle inquired about her friend. "How is Dorie? Have you heard from her lately? I wish she'd write more often."

"Oh, yes, we jest received a letter. Would ya like me ta read a few parts?"

"Please do."

Mr. Cooper's long, thinning hair fell forward, hiding his spectacled face as he bent his head to read the letter that he pulled from his apron pocket.

> *The McClintock's ball attracted guests from all over Charleston.*

He paused to glance at the young ladies, savoring their expressions, and continued.

> *Miss Delaney made her debut in an ivory-colored gown trimmed in . . .*

Elias floundered over the next word.

"May I see?" Annabelle pressed close. Mr. Cooper scratched his bearded chin and reluctantly handed the parchment paper to Annabelle, who scanned over the contents until his stubby finger pointed halfway down the sheet.

"There," he said.

"Rosettes," she sighed.

He snapped the paper back onto the counter.

> *. . . rosettes. She wore genuine pearls and looked exquisite with her black hair fashioned most gracefully atop her head. Of course, all the gentlemen attended her courteously, and I was consumed with jealousy. However, Aunt Adelaide introduced me to an extremely handsome congressman named Brett Powers. The evening turned out to be quite lovely after all.*

"Oh, how dreamy." Annabelle clutched her hands to her breast and swooned. "Real pearls, real gentlemen."

She did not realize that a stranger had earlier entered the store and now observed them from where he browsed. He continued to eavesdrop while the women concluded their shopping.

With sticks of licorice wrapped in tissue paper tucked in a shopping basket, Annabelle hooked her free arm through Claire's, in a light-hearted gesture, and guided her sister toward the door.

"Good morning, ladies."

"Sir?" Annabelle was startled to look up into steel-blue eyes set in a face of granite. As she stared, the statue face turned from stone to liquid, with waves of dimples and creases enveloping a gorgeous smile. The eyes twinkled as if the young man knew something humorous about Annabelle. She blushed and turned to move away.

"Ma'am, may I?" He tipped his hat, displaying shortly cropped brown hair, while the same grin spread across the expanse of his face and his eyes dared her to defy him. "May I introduce myself? My name is Charles Harrison."

Mustering up courage, with Dorie's image flashing in and out of her consciousness, Annabelle responded with a slight curtsy. "Annabelle Larson, and my sister, Claire."

"At your service, I am sure. Where are you headed? May I carry your basket for you?"

"That is very kind, but we are on our way home, and I am sure it would be quite out of your way."

"Ladies, please be assured, it would be a pleasure."

"Perhaps another time, Mr. Harrison."

The young man persisted, "May I call on you, Miss Larson?"

Annabelle retorted with a question of her own. "Will we see you at church on Sunday?"

Charles Harrison admired her quickness and the fire that

shot from those green eyes. The way in which the gorgeous chestnut hair—framing her upturned face—caught the sun's light enchanted him. "Sunday? Why yes, of course. I'll see you on Sunday then, Miss Larson." Another tip of his hat and he disappeared.

With his retreat, Annabelle could not see the smirk on his stony face, hardened by service in the military. He carried a soldier's stance, straight and perfect, but Annabelle only saw a gentleman. As Charles Harrison formulated a plan, he scowled. He had a long ride ahead of him to make it back by Sunday.

six

"It's such a good cause, Reverend," Melanie Caldwell quipped as she bounced the squirmy bundle in her arms.

The preacher reached out to touch the baby's silken cheek. "Luke is excited to present the gift to the orphanage," he said. "His heart is wrapped up in the little ones, and their needs are great." Reverend Emmett Wheeler's face was a looking glass, reflecting his joy of having a son, like Luke, in the ministry.

"Of course, everyone loves the box socials regardless of the cause." Melanie and Reverend Wheeler looked about the room at the anxious young men.

The reverend grinned. "I believe you're right, Melanie. Perhaps I should get the auction started before a few men lose their courage." He chuckled as he straightened his round white collar and moved toward the long wooden benches where the fancy boxes drew the crowd's attention. The many-flavored dishes released tantalizing messages on scented wings, teasing male palates with smells of chicken, pumpkin, freshly baked bread, and cider.

Across the room, Claire clutched Annabelle's sleeve. "I hope Sammy gets my box, but I doubt if he has money to spare."

Annabelle tilted her head sideways to guard the remark meant only for Claire's ears, "You're always interested in the most unlikely creatures."

Claire frowned back at her. "Just because Sammy stutters does not make him a misfit. He is the sweetest boy I know."

"Yes, I know you think so. Now, you'd better wipe that scowl off your face or no one will want to purchase your box." Claire found Annabelle's unsympathetic attitude annoying, but her

36

sister was right—this was not the time to bicker.

The girls scanned the room in search of friends and acquaintances. Annabelle waved to Rebecca Galloway who had moved up in rank, as friends go, when Dorie moved out of the valley. Rebecca and her young brother, James, crossed the room to greet them.

Married women, outfitted in their best calico prints, chatted in small clusters, secure in the knowledge that their husbands would be obtaining their boxes.

Just as the reverend cleared his throat to call the attention of the folks, Annabelle spotted him. Dressed in a flowing white shirt and dark brown pants, the handsome stranger pushed through the crowd, making a straight track toward her.

"Miss Larson, you look lovely. Quickly, which box is yours, before the bidding starts?"

"Mr. Harrison, what a surprise."

"You did invite me this morning." Annabelle colored slightly as she recalled the conversation. When he had appeared at church and continued his pursuit, she had put him off by talking about the box social.

"So I did," she admitted.

"Please don't say you were just trying to get rid of me." Annabelle smiled and trembled when he leaned close and a delicious musky scent filled the air. He whispered, "Now, which is yours?"

Annabelle shifted a few feet away from Rebecca and said in a low tone, "I suppose it won't hurt to tell you. After all, there is no guarantee that you can secure it. And it is for a good cause." Annabelle then described her lunch as a disguised cigar box wrapped in soft blue fabric and secured with white lace knotted about a dried chrysanthemum.

As Charles Harrison slipped away, Rebecca gave Annabelle a searching look. "Where did he come from?"

"I don't know." Annabelle answered honestly. "But I intend

to find out."

Two strapping country boys, Andy Benson and Bart Barnes, eyed the stranger suspiciously. "This city slicker seems to think he can horn in on our territory," Andy told his friend.

Bart straightened and glared at Charles Harrison, who stood within earshot. "Where ya from, mister?"

"Boston, and you?"

"From here. What's your business in Beaver Creek?"

"I don't believe that's any of your affair." The three eyed each other icily. Then the bidding started.

The reverend waved Annabelle's box high in the air for all to see. Thad's departure had opened the door for suitors and she was embarrassed that so many young men bid upon it.

Andy seemed most determined, and she felt her cheeks glow like hot coals as he offered, "One dollar." The room grew quiet, then "Two dollars" echoed from the corner where Charles Harrison stood. Annabelle knew instinctively that he would be able to outbid Andy. Her heart beat wildly until the final offer. The reverend handed the coveted container to Mr. Harrison, who flung a sidelong smirk in Andy's direction. The country lad stood with his hands in his pockets and his bottom lip stuck out like a carp.

The whole thing caused quite a stir. Annabelle fanned her hot cheeks and looked away from the staring faces. Across the room Claire sat with Sammy, and Mattie had joined Kate and Ben. "Predictable creatures," she whispered to Rebecca. "At least Charles Harrison provides a bit of diversion." Rebecca considered her remark and Annabelle noticed a mischievous glint in her friend's eyes.

&

"There you are. I thought you had slipped out the back door." The young Harrison accused Annabelle as he led her to a vacant bench situated against a far wall.

"Nonsense."

"Good."

"Mr. Harrison, what brings you to Beaver Creek?" Annabelle quickly diverted her eyes away from the chrysanthemum tucked into his shirt pocket like a prize for all to see.

"Actually, investments."

"In Beaver Creek?" Annabelle questioned as she placed a crisp linen napkin on her lap and handed an identical match to her dinner partner.

"Precisely. There is a road coming through and I am considering whether to fund it."

"A road?"

Charles reached for a chicken part and nodded, "Ever heard of the National Road?"

"Yes, but . . ." She smiled as she traced the steamy circumference of her mug of apple cider.

Charles wondered what amused her and gently prodded, "But?"

"But surely not, you seem so young. I thought investors were stuffy old men with large stomachs and bulging pockets."

"You have just described my father." They burst into laughter and felt like old friends. Then he unwrapped the tissue paper which held the candy from Cooper's General store. "Licorice, my favorite." The intensity of his gaze insinuated that she had purchased that candy purposely for him. "I am an adventurer at heart so Father allowed me to come in his stead," he said without taking his eyes off her.

"He must have confidence in you."

This pleased Charles and he warmed, "Well, the family inheritance passes to me, so yes, he trusts I'll use good judgment."

"And where is this family?"

"Boston."

Annabelle choked on her food.

"Did I say something wrong?"

"No. I just know someone from there."

"Indeed? Who?"

"His name is Thaddeas Larson."

"Never heard of him. A relative?"

Annabelle sighed, "A cousin."

"I am glad to hear he is not a suitor." Annabelle colored and he continued, "This pumpkin pie is excellent."

"Thank you."

"Now, tell me about yourself, Miss Larson. Have you always lived in Beaver Creek?"

"Mostly. My parents were killed in an Indian raid at Big Bottom. Mattie Larson brought me and my two sisters here to raise."

His eyebrows arched slightly at the mention of Mattie. "I'm sorry. How old were you?"

"Just one. I cannot remember my real parents. Kate remembers them clearly though."

"Kate?"

"Yes, my older sister, married to Ben Wheeler. Over there." She pointed toward her brother-in-law, who was engaged in a serious conversation with the stand-in sheriff, Jude Miller. Annabelle had the distinct impression that they had been talking about her and Charles. They looked her way as she pointed them out, so she feigned a wave. "Uh-oh, guess we got caught." She frowned. "Here they come, I'll introduce you."

Charles jumped to his feet and stiffened as the large freckled man and another, slightly smaller and older with a star pinned to his vest, approached.

"Ben, I would like you to meet Charles Harrison. Charles, this is Ben Wheeler, my brother-in-law, and Jude Miller."

Charles straightened, resuming his soldiering posture, and stretched forth his hand. Ben carefully eyed the man as he shook his hand, "Have we met before? You remind me of someone."

"Not that I remember, sir. But it is a pleasure to do so now."

"Welcome to Beaver Creek, Mr. Harrison."

"Thank you. I am enjoying your town very much."

Jude studied the man who stood before him. Annabelle watched Charles Harrison's face turn to a stony countenance, and wondered why he looked as glum as one headed for the gallows. After some small talk, including an invitation from Ben to visit his farm, the men excused themselves and moved away to resume their private conversation, leaving Annabelle and Charles alone again.

Charles turned to Annabelle, "Would you mind if we step outside for some fresh air?"

She glanced at their supper mess and he bent to lend a hand. When all of the scraps were shoved into the box that Charles had purchased, she reached for her shawl and they moved toward the door.

"May I keep this for a remembrance of this evening?" Charles asked, plucking the flower from his shirt pocket and twirling it between long, slender fingers. Annabelle blushed close to the shade the flower had once been. He slipped his other hand beneath her elbow. The night was black and cool, and his voice sounded like the distant brook—low and musical. "Annabelle."

"Yes." She said in a tone so low that he was not sure if she had replied.

"You're a special young woman," he said, gazing at the star-studded sky. "This has been a pleasant night." He waited for her to look up and watched her face under the moon's light. "May I call on you?"

This time she consented. "Yes, I would like that."

Charles took her hand, his touch firm and gentle, and Annabelle thought for a moment that he was going to kiss it, but he did not. Then like a vapor, he was gone—and she wondered if he was even real.

seven

Sudden drops in temperature teased the trees, producing spectacular color displays. On this particular day, the sun gilded the leaves to brilliance, but the rider did not pause to admire his surroundings. With a message to deliver, he spurred his horse forward until he rounded the bend that revealed Tucker House. As he focused on his destination, he noticed patches of color like flags waving behind the house. Quickly dismounting, the young man strode toward the spot where he found the women doing the wash.

"Telegram! Telegram!"

Mattie dropped the gown she had just removed from the clothesline and snatched the dispatch from the errand boy. When she realized her discourteous behavior, she quickly added, "Thank ya kindly." Ripping it open, she silently read its contents and then exhaled deeply. "Well, that gave my body a scare. 'Tis the sheriff, and he jest wants us to know that everything is fine. Thad is on his way to Boston, and Buck is stoppin' in Dayton for a short visit with Luke Wheeler."

The message carrier saw that all was well and politely made his departure. "Could I git ya a drink?" Mattie called after him when she realized her manners, but he was too far gone and did not hear the invitation.

"When will Buck be home?" Claire asked. Practiced fingers folded clothes, stiff from the sun.

"He didn't say."

"I'm glad he's visiting Luke." Claire was fond of Ben's brother, Luke, who had been her spiritual mentor. She had corresponded with Luke after he left Beaver Creek for college four years earlier. Now he was involved in the orphanage that was a ministry of the Presbyterian Church of Dayton. "In his last letter, I got the impression that he was a bit homesick."

"Is that all Buck said about Thaddeas?" Annabelle complained.

"Jest that he's safely on his way to Boston," Mattie snapped. "Telegrams are always short ya know, too costly otherwise." She grew irritable, for she had been looking forward to Buck's return, and now it was to be delayed. Silently, the three women piled the crisp clothing in their arms as they thought about the message. "Run ahead and heat up the iron, Annabelle," Mattie ordered. Annabelle thought Mattie sounded cross as a general in the army. She resisted the temptation to salute.

Long after the iron had cooled on its spot on the kitchen shelf, and the supper dishes were washed and stacked away in a neighboring niche, the women retired to the sitting room. "Shall I start the fire?" Claire offered with concern for Mattie, who rested with tired feet propped upon a footstool. Freckles, Claire's cat, climbed uninvited onto Mattie's lap.

"Please do," Mattie answered. "My back is achin' and it feels good to sit." She arched like Freckles, working out the kinks.

Claire tossed an armful of logs into the fireplace. She gazed at the fire as it crackled and hissed, then posed a question. "Do you think Thaddeas has to sleep under the stars? Surely, there's not always an inn available."

Annabelle envisioned him with his bedroll, camping with strangers in the night. Her eyes burned as she blinked back tears that threatened to flow. *Thaddeas would not be frightened; he is so strong and dependable,* she reasoned. He always talked about God and faith. Just like everyone else around her. She frowned. This frustrated, yet comforted her. The frustration stemmed from the knowledge that she did not possess or desire this Christian faith that the rest of the family had. The comfort came in leaning on their strength. Thaddeas had been her pillar, always there to protect her, expect the best in her.

"I'm sure Thaddeas is doing jest fine. I worry more about his grief; he seemed so low. But time heals things like that." Mattie's voice faded away as if she were thinking of another time.

Annabelle felt pangs of guilt, knowing she had caused some of his pain.

"Poor Thad," Claire said.

Annabelle shot out of her seat at Claire's remark, unable to listen to another word, for her conscience pricked her sore spot. Mattie and Claire looked at her questioningly, but just then they were interrupted by a knock at the door. They shifted their gaze toward the large, wooden portal. Annabelle pulled the latch with an unsteady touch to receive the unexpected caller.

"Mr. Harrison!"

"Good evening, Miss Larson."

"Please, come in." The ladies jumped to their feet, toppling the footstool, and scaring the cat off Mattie's lap. Annabelle, embarrassed by the confusion, did her best to welcome him.

"Your home is delightful, Miss Larson," he said upon entering. "Why do folks call it Tucker House?"

Annabelle swallowed a lump that stuck like molasses in her throat to explain. "Mattie's name was Tucker before she married the sheriff. Remember, I told you we were adopted? Well, it's been a seamstress shop for many years, and that's the name the townspeople gave it."

Charles digested this information as they seated themselves in the sitting room, and then surprised them by referring back to the beginning of her rejoinder. "Did you know Annabelle's parents, Mrs. Larson?"

Mattie squirmed. "Yes, I did."

"You never told me that before!" Annabelle's voice sounded accusing even in her own ears.

"I-I guess it never came up before. I believe Kate and I have discussed it, though."

"Annabelle's sister?" Charles posed the question, and Mattie nodded. "Was Kate old enough to remember her parents, then?"

"Yes, she remembers the day clear enough. She used to have nightmares 'bout it."

"I imagine you were a comfort to her—the fact that she had a familiar person to go to."

"I wasn't . . . I knew her parents before . . . she was old enough to remember."

"How did you happen to get together with the girls then?"

Mattie frowned at Mr. Harrison. "Enough talk of the past, Mr. Harrison. I'm sure you young folks have more interesting things ta talk about. I was jest about to make some tea when ya came, may I get ya some?" Annabelle wondered about Mattie's sudden burst of energy and looked at the woman with surprise.

"Yes, thank you," Charles replied.

Claire felt awkward and jumped up to assist Mattie, and as soon as they left the room Charles turned his attention toward Annabelle.

"I apologize for Mattie. She misses Buck and is on edge tonight."

"I'm sorry, Annabelle, if I've brought back unpleasant memories."

"When I was fourteen, I was in an accident and lost my memory. Sometimes I wonder if there are things I still don't remember." She blushed, "It's embarrassing."

"Don't be embarrassed. Please go on."

"It was a painful time for me. I didn't like the sympathetic looks my family gave me when I questioned them about things, so I just didn't press them. I should have asked Mattie or Kate more about my parents."

Charles seemed lost in thought and his face turned dismal as a patch of burned stumps. The room grew uncomfortably quiet. Annabelle tried to concentrate on the gentleman sitting beside her and think of some interesting topic to discuss, as Mattie had suggested, but a heaviness remained. She wondered if it stemmed from thinking of her accident, or if her concern for Thad still shadowed her.

"Miss Larson?"

He reached for her hand but she snatched it away.

"Mr. Harrison, I'm . . ."

"Call me Charles."

"Charles, I'm sorry, I'm not very good company tonight. I guess I miss Buck and my cousin about as much as Mattie. We were just talking about them when you came to the door."

"Your cousin?"

"Yes, the one returning to Boston."

"I remember. Well, perhaps tonight is not good. I can call another time."

"Oh, no! I didn't mean that you should leave."

"I think it is for the best."

"Please, Charles, stay."

"Another time, when you are not preoccupied." His voice sounded harsh, and he shot a withering look her way as he rose to his feet.

"Charles, wait. I'm really sorry." She rambled on, apologizing as she pursued him toward the door. He turned abruptly and she bumped into his chest. They stared at each other momentarily, and then his face took on a look of condescending amusement.

"Give Mrs. Larson my apologies for not taking tea. Good night, Miss Larson."

"Please . . . call me Annabelle."

"Annabelle." He whispered as he brushed her pink flannel cheek with his finger in the same manner someone might treat a small child.

After she closed the door, she stomped her foot. "Well, I never saw the like! What an impossible man!"

eight

Buck Larson arrived in Dayton on the fourth of October, five days trail beaten. From the Golden Lamb, they had traveled on the washboard-rough Old Military Road. In Cincinnati, they tarried a full day until Thaddeas got passage on a vessel via the Ohio River destined for Zane's Trace. After an emotional departure Buck, struck by impulse, sent a telegram to Mattie that he was stopping in Dayton, another two-day trip on the Mad River road.

ᵌ

Dayton, the city where many rivers come together—the Miami, Stillwater, Mad, and Wolf Creek—had grown so much since his last visit that Buck hardly recognized it. Iron-tired wagons grated noisily over the paving stones, and children dodged in and out among the merchants gathered on the street.

Buck pulled his red kerchief from his vest pocket and wiped his brow. Then he made his way to Main and Water Streets and dismounted in front of the Newcom Tavern. A clammy kiss of cold air arose from the river and enveloped him outside the two-story log building, which at various times served as courthouse, church, school, and post office. He opened the bulky wooden door and entered, boots creaking on the warped wooden floor. A bushy-haired man with a broom-bottom mustache and white apron greeted Buck, leading him to a tiny table to be served.

After his thirst and hunger were adequately satisfied, he inquired, "Where's the orphanage?"

"Ya mean the asylum?"

Buck's face flinched. The expression sounded callous—too harsh. The man with tumbleweed hair seemed indifferent as he gave directions, and Buck paid him and left.

The orphanage was located on the outskirts of town on a parcel of land sheltered several miles from the river bank. The thought crossed Buck's mind that it was something to be thankful for; at least the air was not as chilly. He tied his mount at the hitching post outside the stone building that expansed before him. It was long and narrow, and reminded him of a large bunkhouse like the one he had seen on Tanner Matthew's place, a prominent rancher in Beaver Creek.

He banged on the door, and it swung open to reveal a blond young man of six feet, lean and sturdy. Astonishment covered the boyish face. "Sheriff Larson! Buck." Luke pulled the sheriff into an embrace and pumped his hand in a rush of excitement. Released and held at arm's length for inspection, Buck noticed a small crowd gathering about them.

Peeping eyes, huge grins, and thin bodies etched simultaneously into Buck's consciousness. Luke followed his glance and then motioned for the small tykes to come forward. "Come, meet my friend, Sheriff Larson."

One boy of about seven boldly stepped forward from the huddle. "You a real sheriff?"

"Yes, lad, but you need not be afraid. I'm here to visit Mr. Wheeler."

"Mr. Luke," the lad corrected him shyly.

Buck chuckled. "What is your name, Son?"

"Barnabus. But you kin call me Barney." That tickled the smaller children and they giggled and squirmed in turn when Luke led Buck to the group for introductions.

There were fourteen orphans, of ages varying from eighteen months to fourteen years. They were dressed in hand-me-down clothes, clean and mended. Luke guided Buck down a long hallway and entered the kitchen—dark, bleak, but warm from the blackened oven-fireplace.

A yellow-haired woman, young and curvaceous, with smooth skin the color of apricots, looked up from her work. She was introduced as Mrs. Catherine. Buck also met her counterpart, Mr. Jesse. Their surname was Murdock, but the children dispensed of such formalities, attaching titles to given names.

The sheriff enjoyed his visit, though the children tugged his heartstrings. He asked Luke about little Barney Forbes, his favorite.

"He is one of five children," Luke explained. "Abigail is fourteen, Brooke twelve, Hank ten. Then, there is your Barney, who is seven, and his younger brother Lonnie, five. Their pa plunged to his death in a wagon accident, coming west. The mother also died along the trail from lung fever. The wagon master brought them as far as Dayton, and the orphanage took them in."

"How sad."

"Yes. Actually, Abigail is quite mature, and could probably raise them if they had a home. But you see, there was no place for them to go."

The tragedies of the youngsters turned Buck's thoughts homeward, to the town he sheriffed. Being Beaver Creek's troubleshooter meant twenty-four-hour duty protecting its citizens, anticipating and avoiding crises. A sense of urgency overwhelmed him. He needed to get back to his charge.

Early the next morning, cutting his visit a day short, he made his farewells and stuffed a letter Luke had written to his father, the reverend, in his vest pocket. Then he headed home.

❧

The afternoon sun toasted Annabelle's cheeks and made her drowsy. Expelling a happy sigh, she threw off the temptation to dismount and take a nap in the piles of leaves strewn along the way. She enjoyed horseback riding and was grateful Sheriff Larson had taught her to ride after he came to Tucker House to live.

Annabelle guided her mount, Dusty, slowly along the dirt road and thought how good it was to get away from home where Buck's absence gnawed at Mattie, making her mopish. It sickened her to watch Claire chirp about like a mother robin, doing extra things to cheer Mattie, and made her wonder why Claire was such a do-gooder, even worse than Kate.

A squirrel darted across the road and scurried to a high limb of an oak tree that canopied the roadway. It scolded her as she rode beneath. Annabelle tried to spot the creature in the maze of twisted gray limbs until the straining action put a crick in her neck. When her gaze returned to the trail, to her surprise, a horse and rider fast approached.

She straightened to full height in the saddle, absentmindedly tidying her riding habit as best she could with one hand. Her hair, which was pulled back in a ribbon, sprung out in various directions where stubborn strands had worked free.

Thus, when Charles Harrison caught her vision, Annabelle's natural-looking beauty beckoned. He reined in his horse, for he was going at a brisker clip than she.

"Good afternoon, Annabelle. What a pleasant surprise," he puffed.

"Charles." Annabelle nodded, while holding Dusty in check.

"Riding becomes you. You look beautiful." He could not tell if she blushed from his words or if the sun had burned her cheeks. "Are you headed someplace special?"

"No, just riding. I was about to turn around and head back." As soon as she spoke the words she was sorry. It sounded like she was fishing for an invitation, and she did not even think she liked this moody person.

"I was thinking about a rest," he said. "It is so lovely here."

"It isn't far to the creek. It is breathtaking there."

"I would love to see the spot. Would you care to dismount and show me?"

"Well, I don't know, I should be getting back." She looked over her shoulder toward Tucker House and recalled how boring it was to watch Claire console Mattie. "On second thought, a small excursion is exactly what I need."

Charles' face registered surprise as he regarded her

carefully—a beautiful, copper-haired maiden looking for adventure. He threw back his head and chuckled. Then all in one motion he was off his horse and coming to her side.

Annabelle dismounted with butterfly grace and allowed him to fasten their horses.

"This way, race you," she tossed the challenge into the wind.

"Hey, wait! I don't know where we're going." With longer strides he soon caught up to her. Panting and giggling, they ran side by side until they reached the banks of the Beaver Creek, which meandered in and out through the wooded brush. Annabelle dropped to her knees.

"I've wanted to do this all afternoon," she gasped.

"What?" He asked while settling at her side.

"Sink into these leaves. They smell like autumn."

"Do they? Let me see." He scooped up an armful and buried his face into the scratchy, brittle flakes while inhaling deeply. "Indeed they do." While yet speaking, he tossed them into the air above her head and they deposited over her like a haystack, tickling her face and clinging to her hair and clothes.

"Oh! You scoundrel!" She shook her head vigorously, and for a moment he thought she might be angry, but she burst into a fit of giggles.

"Here, let me help." Charles rolled over on his side and tenderly picked tree crumbs out of her thick tresses. Her laughter subsided as she gazed into his mirth-filled eyes. The next thing she knew he had lifted her chin upwards and placed a light kiss on her lips.

"Annabelle." He breathed her name.

She gave him a playful push and moved out of his reach, where she scrambled to her feet and brushed off her riding skirt. He lay there looking at her and she dared to offer him her hand. Pulling him to his feet, she ordered, "Come along, Charles, there is much more to be seen."

"Yes, madam."

They departed hand in hand.

nine

Buck swung Mattie round and round until she squealed, breathless. Annabelle and Claire watched from the porch, laughing as the two of them behaved like newlyweds. When the couple finally approached, arm in arm, the girls embraced the sheriff, each in turn.

"Welcome home, Buck," Annabelle said as she released the giant man.

"It is good to be back." Buck's voice was husky.

The women buzzed around him like bees over a honeycomb. Once inside, Mattie set a mug of coffee in front of him and asked, "Hungry?"

"Just a snack, if you have something."

Mattie shined an apple on her skirt and handed it to him. "Now, tell us all about your trip."

"How is Thaddeas?" Annabelle asked.

"Did you see any Indians?" Claire wondered.

"Whoa, one question at a time." The sheriff raised his thick, leathery hand to stop the attack. "Thad held up, a bit haggard from the first leg of travel—but doing good enough. One of the hardest things I ever did was say good-bye to the lad. There was a group headed in his direction, so he won't be traveling alone, which is safer. As for his sorrow, that will take some time."

"Poor Thad," Claire sniffed. "You're sure he's safe then, from the Indians and all?"

"He's in the Lord's care," Mattie pointed out.

"We need to continue to pray for him, daily." Buck studied their faces. "The Indians are up to something. We met a

52

Lieutenant Brooks from Fort Wayne under the command of Captain William Wells. They believe we're on the verge of an Indian uprising. The captain sent him to scout out information on Chief Tecumseh and his brother the Prophet. . . Mattie!"

Buck quickly reached out to steady his wife, who had turned pale and limp. "Are you all right? Please, don't be frightened."

"I-I'm fine," she protested.

"I'm sure we'll be safe here, so close to town." He assured her as he patted her hand.

"Tecumseh!" Annabelle remembered her friend mentioning that name. "Rebecca Galloway told me about him. Surely, he is harmless. He's a frequent visitor in their home. Why, she even reads to him."

Buck scowled, considering her comments. Then she added as an afterthought, "It's almost like she's sweet on him."

"Don't be ridiculous," Claire rolled her eyes. "He's an Indian."

"When did you have such a long talk with Rebecca?" Buck asked.

"At the box social, Sunday night."

Claire piped up, "Speaking of the social, Annabelle has a new beau."

"Oh, Claire, stop it!"

Claire's face took on a peachy glow as she continued to tease her sister. "Charles Harrison, a gentleman from Boston."

"He's new to the valley. Won't be stayin'," Mattie offered. "He's thinkin' about fundin' the new National Road."

"I thought it was to be government funded," Buck said. "How did you meet this stranger?"

"He's not exactly a stranger. He comes to church. Anyway, we're just friends."

"He bought Annabelle's boxed lunch," Claire giggled.

Mattie took pity on Annabelle and changed the subject. "The reverend is sending the money to Luke's orphanage."

Buck chuckled. "It's not exactly Luke's orphanage, but the children sure look up to him. He's a fine young man."

"Tell us about him, and the children," Claire begged.

"There are fourteen children. Such sad stories! There's a set of brothers, little tykes whose folks and siblings died of typhoid; another family of three, deserted by their ma and pa because there were too many mouths to feed." He thought of little Barney and his brothers and sisters. It was too painful; he did not mention them. "The children are loved now. Pity is, it could be too late for some of them. You see, some were alone or abused for years before the Murdocks heard about them.

"Catherine and Jesse Murdock parent them like they were their own, and Luke spends every afternoon with them. He helps with some of the teaching—they have schooling there at the home."

Buck rubbed his chin and nodded thoughtfully, "Yep, Luke is doing good. His faith in God is strong as a buffalo and, along with the Murdocks, he is doing the Lord's work by providing those younguns with love and care."

Claire clung like moss to every word Buck said. "I wish I could help. Do you think I could?"

"Well, I don't know, Claire." The question took Buck by surprise. Annabelle stared in disbelief at her sister.

"Claire! Are you crazy?"

"We were orphans, weren't we? The Lord provided us with a home. There's a scripture I've been thinking about. Let me read it." Claire brushed past Annabelle in a hurry to find her Bible. In moments she returned. "Here it is, Matthew 10:8: 'Freely ye have received, freely give.' I like that. I think that's the way it's meant to be."

"Are you telling me that God caused our folks to be killed so that we can go help orphans?"

"No, of course not. But when you can feel other folks' pain, you can help them better."

"Well, Claire, you do that enough for the two of us."

"Girls, we can talk about this later," Mattie interrupted. "We'll give it some thought. Right now it's time for supper, and I'll need ya both in the kitchen."

"Oh, Mattie?" Buck called.

"Yes?"

"Do you know anything about a note that was left on my desk at the office, something about another prowler at Ben's?"

"What? Why, no."

"Hm. Wonder what it's about."

❧

Annabelle's eighteenth birthday came and went in October. The weeks sped by as she spent many hours with Charles. Riding together had become a regular occurrence since the day they had met accidentally by the creek.

Annabelle battled pendulum emotions. Sometimes she soared in the clouds, romancing with Charles, but most often she sank into depression, unable to get her mind off Thaddeas. Unconsciously, she weighed the differences between the two men.

Unpredictable Charles Harrison swept Annabelle off her feet with suave charm one moment, and turned cold as ice the next. Yet he possessed all of the things she coveted—a good family, wealth, charm, and looks. Many nights she lay awake, considering him. He was attracted to her, but lacked any feelings of commitment. She asked herself, *Would he propose marriage? Is that what I want? Would Thaddeas approve?*

Thad had sent two telegrams. The first came from the Spread Eagle Tavern in Philadelphia on October 17th, saying he was fine. She worried about his safety until his second telegram arrived on November 4th. "Arrived safe, Boston." Her heart remained heavy even with this assurance and she missed him sorely.

ten

Thad shook his dark, curly head as he looked about him and hastened his gait. The stench of swine overpowered him. Instinctively, his nose wrinkled its protestation. Boston, referred to as the "swineless city" because the creatures were not allowed to run loose like they were in most cities, was not true to its nickname today.

A pig drover, bringing hogs to market, created a general disturbance, maneuvering his herd through the main thoroughfare. Dogs yipped at the strays, which squealed and staggered back into the waddling procession.

When he rounded the corner at Tremont Street, leaving the confusion behind, Thad loosened his necktie in a frustrated effort to resist the phantom that accompanied him wherever he went. Annabelle was ever on his mind. Her words echoed through his memory, "And what is wrong with wealth?" He had to admit that it was a great deal more pleasant than the poverty he encountered in parts of Boston.

After living in luxury for the past two weeks, Thad wondered if he had been too hard on Annabelle. After all, he had never been in need himself. But then neither had Annabelle. He grew weary of his thoughts, and determined for the hundredth time not to let her memory control him.

He wanted to clear his mind, so on an impulse, he turned to his brother. "Leon, where does Mary Beth work?"

"Why, she is a dairy maid."

"I know that, but where?"

"Oh, on Bromfield and Washington."

"Really? Could we swing by there?"

"Of course; she'd like that."

Leon, an older version of Thaddeas, possessed the same raven hair, soft brown eyes, strong physique, and gentle personality. However, he was more suited to city life, a gentleman at the word's best. He could not understand Thad's infatuation with the western wilderness, pursuing new frontiers and dealing with Indians and backwoodsmen.

Plagued with loneliness and worry, Leon had insisted that Thaddeas return for the reading of the will. Hoping Thad's call to adventure would diminish once he laid eyes on Boston again, Leon planned for his brother to join him in the family business.

Now Leon was glad to accommodate Thad. His younger brother's restlessness and despondency since arriving in Boston troubled Leon. Mary Beth Edwards. If that was what it took to interest Thad, well . . .

They turned and walked south, two streets out of their normal trek, and soon approached a large brick building where the dairy women put in their long hours. The huge room they entered smelled musty and looked bleak except for the stone fireplace that graced the very center of the expanse. Here, the girls gathered periodically to warm themselves.

Intrigued, Thad and Leon observed the various stages of the process. They noticed an adjoining spring house that appeared cold and damp, where shallow pans separated the cream. At the opposite wall, some women churned, and others kneaded and pressed cream into a solid consistency, using their hands. There, they spotted her.

"Mary Beth!" Thad waved his arm in greeting.

A slender, light-haired girl with turquoise eyes patted a pale lump with delicate hands. As she recognized her visitors, a smile formed on the thin smooth lips and lit up her creamy face.

Thad grinned broadly as he crossed the vast distance of the

room with Leon upon his heels. Mary Beth and Thaddeas had renewed their acquaintance when she had accompanied her mother on a recent visit to the Larson home. Mary Beth had changed considerably in the five years Thad had lived in Ohio.

Both attended the Old North Church on Hull Street and held many things in common. Miss Edward's family occupied the same class as Thad's, that of the wealthy merchant class. The young woman was gentle-hearted, yet not bashful. She loved adventure and could always be found out "doing" something. Just so, Mary Beth recently had hired on as a dairy maid to fill in for a sick friend who attended her church, so the girl would not lose her job.

Since his return to Boston, Thad had noticed Mary Beth's attentive manner on the occasions when they had met at church functions, which did much to restore his torn ego. He found her warm and sympathetic, like a soothing ointment for his fractured state of mind. It felt good to lean on someone strong in spirit. Today he needed her presence.

"Such gallant callers, I am honored." Mary Beth tilted her head in a slight bow, but the words were not meant to mock. Then she smiled brilliantly and motioned with her arm. "See! Is it not amazing?"

"Indeed," Thaddeas agreed. "So many girls in one place. I like it very much."

"Oh, you!" Mary Beth's head bobbed with amusement. "Come. Let me show you how they make cheese." Her enthusiasm was infectious as they toured the dairy. She explained how they preserved the cow's stomach lining that had enzymes to solidify milk into curds. The women squeezed the milk through cheesecloth, then compressed it in a cheese press. They peered through a long, open window into a room where shelves of cheese aged.

When they completed the tour, she impulsively asked, "Now, what really brought you boys around?" Leon blushed as Mary

Beth's gaze rested on him, and he nodded toward his brother, so she turned to Thad for the answer.

Thaddeas moved close so she alone could hear his voice which, while low, echoed in the huge room. "I've been thinking about you, wondering if you would mind if I came calling?"

Her voice, soft and faintly reverberating, was like a caress. "I'd like that."

"Tonight?" Thad asked.

She smiled at him in wonder. "I would be delighted."

"What time would be convenient?"

"Seven o'clock. Oh, no." Her face took on a look of disappointment as she reconsidered, "I promised Mother to take supper to a family that lives on our street. I am sorry."

"Can't I go along?"

"Of course." She brightened. "If you like."

"Good, I'll pick you up in our carriage. Seven o'clock."

"Very well. Thank you, Thaddeas." Every letter of her words hinged on respect.

"Good day, Mary Beth."

"Thanks for dropping by, boys."

"Bye, Mary Beth," Leon called while making giant strides to keep up with his brother, who hurried for the door.

"Nice girl." Thad whistled as they walked past the bare trees lining Bromfield Street. Unconsciously, he plucked off a single leaf, nearly the last of its kind, hanging on tenaciously against frost's assault. He released it carelessly, and it floated downward to the ground. "Nice girl," he repeated.

Leon suppressed a grin.

Feeling Leon's amusement, Thad cleverly diverted his brother's attention, "Look, Leon!" He slapped his brother across the chest. "The potter! Let's surprise Mother with something new!"

"Good idea."

Amelia Larson, a stout, yet elegant, woman with black hair coiled about a pleasant face, turned the smooth, cool vase, admiring the piece at various angles, then set it aside and patted Thad's hand. "Thank you, Darling. It's a lovely vase."

Thad looked at the plump, soft hand resting on his, cuffed in lace, expressing warmth and caring. Then he considered the sweet, familiar face of his mother, whose eyes now misted. "I want you to be happy, Son."

"I know, Mother. And I am."

"No, I would not call it happiness. Perhaps testing or confusion?"

"You are wise." He squeezed her fingertips.

"But what is so troubling?"

"I love the West. The folks in the Ohio Valley are different from the people in Boston. They work hard and enjoy the small things in life that we take for granted. They need to depend on each other because of destiny itself—weather, Indians, wild animals, cold, hunger—makes them a caring lot. They're honest and simple." His mother did not interrupt, yet tried to imagine the Ohio settlers as he painted their description.

"Your cousins, they are lovely girls?"

"Yes, Mother. Kate, of course, is married. She is beautiful, perfection in all ways." Amelia smiled at what must be an exaggeration, but he did not notice. "Claire is pretty on the inside; she is kindness personified. They are Christians. Then, there is Annabelle." How could he describe her?

"Tell me about Annabelle." Instantly, Amelia ascertained that this was the lass who caused Thad's confusion.

"Annabelle. She is quite stunning—no, absolutely gorgeous— full of life . . ." He paused to find proper words to portray the woman he loved, " . . . beautiful as a spring day and deadly as a rattlesnake." He sighed, "She's a red-headed spitfire, irresistible, unreasonable, and I am afraid, not a believer."

"And you love this girl?"

"Ah, Mother, yes. And she will be the death of me." Amelia waited patiently until he continued. "I've loved her since I laid eyes on her, but she was too young, only fourteen. I waited patiently for her to mature, which she did physically. But she's still a child at heart. Before I got your letter saying Father had died, I asked her to marry me. She turned me down flat. I asked her again before I left, but she said no."

"I am sorry. She must be a foolish girl." So recently experiencing the loss of one she loved deeply, Amelia sympathized with her son.

"She has dreams high as the sky and they are everything to her. Annabelle covets all that money and city life can provide."

"I do not understand, then, what is the problem? Doesn't she know you can provide all of that for her? Surely, from the reading of the will, you realize you are a very wealthy young man. Why, with our investments, and. . ."

"Mother," Thad interrupted, "I did not tell her. I wanted her love."

"I see."

Thad scowled, "Of course, I did not even realize how affluent we were, until the will was read. It is ironic." A dreamy smile froze Amelia's face. "What is it, Mother?"

"I was thinking of Mary Beth. The two of you are very much alike. You both could have anything money can buy, yet stubbornly push to make your own way." She considered their similar convictions, "And you share a strong commitment to serve Jesus."

"You sound like a matchmaker, Mother."

"Do I? I'm sorry."

"Actually, I have been weighing those very thoughts. As a matter of fact, I'm calling on her tonight."

Amelia's face lit, glowing like the oil lamp on the nearby parlor stand, while Thaddeas reddened several shades lighter than the scarlet velvet draperies hanging across the room.

Thaddeas' mother fingered the lace-edged handkerchief on her lap. "Thad, we want what is best for you. Your brother does not really need you in the shop, but he wants you there. Of course, there is plenty of room for you in the business. Leon would go to great lengths to keep you here in Boston, and I hope you decide to stay with us. But, it must be your decision."

The servant girl entered the parlor, "Ma'am, dinner is served."

"Thaddeas, shall we join your brother?"

"Yes, I'm starved."

eleven

Mattie Larson's black-booted feet stepped off the distance between Tucker House and Cooper's General Store. She shuffled thoughts as she walked, concentrating on her shopping list: two brown spools for Mrs. Jenning's gown, cinnamon for Thanksgiving pies, and she wanted to look at the woolen stockings.

She lifted her skirts high to step up onto the wooden walkway that edged the shops in Beaver Creek. The timbers had weathered rough, yet she managed to keep her clothing off the splintered edges. A waft of autumn breeze roused a dust devil and she paused to watch the swirling leaves.

As she shifted her gaze to the folks that occupied the shops and roadways, a tall figure across the street caught her eye. Unnerved, she ducked behind a post and watched. The brown-haired military man made long strides toward the Lone Wolf, the local tavern.

Mattie clutched the breast of her winter cape, digging her fingernails into its deep pile. *Wade! It is you!* Years had molded the boyish face into a stern, sober one, yet she recognized the man. Her heart somersaulted, just like twenty-three years earlier. What should she do? Frantically, she rushed into Cooper's General Store.

Elias Cooper noticed the breathless entrance and pale, stricken face. Very little slipped by him, and he wondered why the stranger, a lieutenant, had frightened her.

"Mattie, somethin' wrong?"

"No!" She snapped. "I'm jest needin' some notions." She drew her torso to full height, forced a smile, and marched

63

trembling legs to the back of the store. There, hidden from view, she leaned against the rack of many colored threads to steady herself. Her finger twirled the soft spools, and she thumbed a brown one loose from its peg.

"Dear God, what does this mean? What am I to do?" she prayed. Then a picture flashed, and she relived the scene, four years earlier, of a snowy December morning in Buck's office. It was where he had proposed, and she had told him her life's story. She quickly collected the other items on her list. She must talk to Buck.

Moments later, she entered the room where she had bared her soul that other day. The furnishings remained the same. She saw the stone fireplace and its wooden-beamed mantel supporting Buck's old holster. The things that Buck cherished— from his deer antlers to his bearskin rug—and the familiar smells of leather and coffee stirred her, and she flung herself into his arms.

"Darling, what's wrong?" Buck scooped her into his all-encompassing embrace and waited until she could speak.

Her husband's arms felt strong and protective, his chest warm and comforting just like his unreserved love. Mattie succumbed to sobs, "I-I don't deserve you."

"Don't be silly, Mattie. Tell me. What is it?"

"I love ya, Buck. Ya know I do."

Buck smiled. "I'll never tire of those words. I waited so long to hear them." He stroked her back, encouraging her to continue while a knot constricted in his stomach, for it was not like her to respond hysterically. He pulled out a chair for each of them as he mentally prepared himself.

"Remember the day ya proposed, and I told ya about my past?" Buck nodded, and she hung her head in shame, stumbling for words. "I told ya about gettin' pregnant when I was young without bein' married."

"Mattie, there's no need to go over this."

"I never named the father."

"And now you want to tell me?"

Mattie nodded her head. "Lieutenant Wade Brooks."

Buck sat motionless, taking in the meaning. Putting a name to the fact cut deep. His stomach lurched, yet he remained calm.

"Why are you telling me this now, Mattie?"

"I don't know. It jest seemed the right thing to do. I saw him in town a minute ago. I don't know why he's here. Ya mentioned meetin' him at the Golden Lamb. It was the first I knew he was a lieutenant."

Then Buck remembered Mattie's reaction the day he returned from Dayton, her pale face at the mention of the man's name. How foolish he had been to think she was frightened of the Indians. "Did you talk to him?" he asked.

"No! And I don't want to, but since he turned up, I wanted ya to know, firsthand, from me."

"Thank you, Mattie. It doesn't change anything between us. That's the important thing." He patted her hand. "We'll just take this one step at a time, and see it through together."

੩

The wind brushed Annabelle's curved form, billowing her riding skirt and whipping her hair. Even Dusty's mane tossed about like waves of corn silk. The gallop and gale invigorated Annabelle, and she was hard put to rein in at the designated meeting place—the same spot where she had been meeting Charles for weeks.

She smiled, satisfied that she had arrived early enough to arrange her hair before he showed. Just a trace of a musky scent lingered in the air, the same as Charles used. Instantly, her curiosity was aroused. Then she noticed a paper flapping in the breeze, from a tall beech tree. She dismounted, tied Dusty to a bush, and investigated. It must be from Charles. Snatching the note, she read:

Annabelle,

Another time, another place, and I could have loved you. But that is not to be our destiny. Duty calls me away, just as it brought us together. Please do not hate me. I'll remember you forever, my copper-haired country maiden.

Fondly,
Charles

"Of all the nerve! I cannot believe this! *Country maiden!*" Annabelle crushed the paper and threw it to the ground in disgust. Then she stomped about flailing her arms like a mad hen, muttering loathsome things about Boston gentlemen, ending with, "They think they are so high and mighty, running off to their precious Boston! Everyone I love disappears, back to that horrid place. Thaddeas, I hate you! Why did you leave?"

Hurt and confused, she stooped, picked up the crumpled note, and settled on a nearby log. It was a place where she and Charles had sat together many times. She carefully ironed out the wrinkles with her palm and reread its contents. "Fondly, Charles." Cupping her face in her hands, she succumbed to tears.

❧

Attired in proper military fashion, Charles Harrison dismounted and saluted his lieutenant.

"Sir."

"Corporal Harrison. What is your report?"

"Confirmed. Her maiden name was Tucker, just like you thought. Their ages, twenty-two, eighteen, and sixteen, Sir."

The lieutenant stared across the brown meadow, perfect jaws clenched under eyes shadowed with heaviness. Then he relaxed and nodded. "As I suspected. The evidence is sufficient. No more prowling around for you. Consider this assignment finished. Let's mount and ride together to the fort. Tell me all you know, Corporal."

twelve

The Larson wagon appeared just as the Thanksgiving bird that turned on Reverend Wheeler's fireplace spit was roasted to perfection. Luke, who was home for the holiday, rushed to greet the guests.

"Luke! It's so good to see you!" Mattie embraced the brawny young man who towered over her, then held him at arm's length. "Jest let me look at ya. Healthy and glowin' with the Lord's blessin'."

"Hello, Luke," Buck greeted the young Wheeler, who returned his iron handshake.

"Your visit meant a lot to me, Buck. Lifted my spirits tremendously."

"It was my pleasure, though it gave me a lot to think about."

Luke gave Annabelle a gentle squeeze. "You've become a charming young woman."

Annabelle blushed under his inspection, "Welcome home, Luke."

Then he spied his favorite, shyly hanging back. Luke held out his arms and Claire flew into them. Through their correspondence, he knew more about this young woman's thoughts, feelings, and struggles than did her own family. Suddenly aware of this, Claire turned bashful. Luke assessed the situation and released her, taking in the tender age—twelve when he left, fifteen at their last meeting, now a budding sixteen. He tried to ease her jitters.

"I am especially pleased to see you, Claire. I have so much to tell you."

"You do?"

"Yes, and you encouraged me with your faithful letters." Claire soon warmed under his reassuring manner and her devotion quickened when he asked her about Freckles, the cat he had given her as a gift several years earlier.

Mary Wheeler interrupted the eye-watering homecoming by calling them to dinner. Eleven gathered around the Thanksgiving table. Emmett glowed with satisfaction at having his entire family present.

"Let us pray," he bellowed. "Thank you, gracious Father, for each loved one here today, for the labor of their hands and hearts, for this bounteous food set before us, and mostly for your precious son, Jesus. Amen."

Amens chorused the room, and then the place charged with the buzz of chatter and the scraping of utensils against pewter plates. "Tell us about the work you are doin', Luke." Mattie pointed her fork in his direction, giving him the floor.

"Where do I start?" The young man scratched his straw-covered head.

"With the children," Claire nearly burst with enthusiasm. Expectant eyes round and blue, not willing to miss a word he had to say, watched his every move.

"All right. Cody and Gabe Calton are the youngest—eighteen months and three years. Their folks died with typhoid last spring so they've been in the orphanage for about seven months. The home consists mostly of older children, because babies usually get snapped up by relatives or childless families. I'm surprised this pair hasn't."

Luke paused to look around the circle of friends and relatives. Noting their attentiveness, he continued. "Adorable tykes, but it makes things extra tough, caring for a little one with so much to be done at the orphanage—schooling, cooking, clothing, and care. Of course, the older ones pitch in."

Kate placed her hand across her mouth to stifle a sob and kept her eyes glued to her plate. She felt Ben's sympathetic gaze and could not look at her husband for fear of breaking down in front of the family.

"There is one boy that I wish you would keep in your prayers. He is the oldest, fourteen." Luke jabbed at his peas with his fork, scooting them around his plate as he spoke. "Name is Adam Parks. Beaten and left for dead when he was about nine by his ma's new husband, he lived on the streets in Philadelphia until he hired on with a hard man that worked him excessively and also battered the poor boy.

"Adam ran away and ended up in Dayton, where he has been with us for about a year. Last week the blacksmith took him on as an indentured servant. He's a decent man, but Adam doesn't trust people. I pray that he won't run away and end up God knows where, but that he will give it a chance. . ." Luke choked up and could not continue. "I planned to stop in and visit him, but I made this trip home just when he needed me."

"He's in the Lord's hands, Son. God wants to give us the desires of our hearts. He knows yours, and we're grateful for this visit."

"I want to help, Luke. What can I do?" Claire stood to her feet, and all eyes fastened on her.

Her plea touched Luke's heart. James and Frank had listened attentively and now Frank nudged Mary. "Ma. Christmas is coming up. Could we do something for the children?"

"Why, that's a wonderful idea! What could we do, Luke?" Mattie joined in the excitement.

"Let's go to Dayton; let's visit them," Claire suggested. She nearly danced, hoping to see the home and get involved.

"Luke?" His father questioned and silence hovered over the group as they waited for the response.

A huge grin birthed beneath quivering lips to tickle Luke's newly-grown mustache. His sea-blue eyes lit like candles and the crinkles in his forehead indicated pleasure. "I-I don't know what to say."

"I say, let's start planning." Buck set his fist on the table like a judge's gavel and a babbling of ideas erupted.

Frank interrupted, "The kids need gifts."

Mattie ordered, "Luke, have Mrs. Murdock send us a list of things they'll be needin' right away, when you git back."

Annabelle's brow creased in thought. It seemed to her that things were getting out of hand. *Sure the children are sad little ragamuffins, but why do I have to get involved? Where is my life headed?* She answered her own question. *Surely in the wrong direction—visiting the poorhouse itself. Oh heavens! Everything is out of control,* and she twisted the napkin on her lap between two clenched fists.

ﾑ

As usual, Kate and Annabelle sought each other out for a bosom talk. Just now, they walked through Emmett Wheeler's apple orchard. Though they were fully cloaked, the air pierced them, stinging their faces a raw pink. Kate's mittened hand patted her sister's arm. "You're going through some hard times, aren't you?"

Annabelle's reply spewed forth like a volcano eruption. "Charles jilted me. You'll never believe it. He left a note hanging on a tree. Said he'd always remember his . . ." She spit out the last two words, ". . . country maiden."

Kate knew the pet name had injured her sister's pride. "Did you love him?"

"No." Annabelle kicked at the ground.

Kate, noting the quick retort and angry response, asked, "Are you sure?"

"I'm sure. I-I love Thaddeas."

Kate clapped her padded hands. "I knew it." Then she hugged Annabelle.

"It's no use. He's gone."

"It's not too late. I know! Send him a telegram."

Annabelle giggled. "A telegram?"

"Sure, it would be so romantic."

Green eyes fired and copper curls bobbed as Annabelle began to scheme. "A love telegram. I'll do it!" The girls stood in one spot, drafting the message, puffs of vapor shooting upward at each new idea, while rubbing their hands and stomping their feet to keep warm.

Annabelle turned toward Kate. "Thanks so much. I feel better. Ready to go in? I'm about frozen."

"Just one thing, first. I haven't talked to Ben, but I'm going to adopt those babies."

"What babies?"

"Cody and Gabe, the little boys Luke described. That is, if Ben is willing."

"Kate, I don't know what to say."

"Pray about it, Annabelle," her sister pressed.

"I can't promise that. You know I'm not big on praying."

"Start. It means so much to me."

"I'm sure Ben will understand. Two babies, already grown, that would sure change things around here."

Kate beamed and they headed back to the house with their spirits soaring in anticipation.

thirteen

Taking a reprieve from the blurry numbers dancing before his bloodshot eyes, Thaddeas uprighted his taut body, then peered out the foggy window, clearing a circle of vision with his shirt sleeve. The leather shop was grossing large profits, and he would have to speak with Leon about securing new investments.

Surprised, he noticed the late afternoon sky had blackened while he had pored over ledger pages. The heavens rumbled warnings and the clouds churned, prompting him to prepare for home before the storm's fury hit the city. He set about to put his desk in order when a chill rushed across his back and ruffled the papers he had worked to straighten. Just as suddenly, the door banged directly behind him, causing him to jump.

"Telegram for Thaddeas Larson."

"Here!" Thaddeas waved to the lanky youth who called his name while he took in the bundled body and woolen-scarfed head.

"The wind is stirring up, sir. Sorry to startle you."

Thad winced as he exchanged the telegram for a coin and wondered what the communication could contain. His last wire had been bad news. He remembered to thank the lad just before he left, and shivered as another mighty gust blitzed through the office.

Easing himself back into the padded chair behind his polished desk, he utilized the armrests and stared at the envelope. "Oh, Lord," he prayed, "prepare my heart." He tore open the seal and pulled out the contents. Greedily, he devoured the message, all at once, then digested it word for word.

> *Dearest Thaddeas,*
> *Make me yours. I love you. Boston suits fine.*
> *Annabelle.*

He ruffled his bushy black hair with thick trembling hands, reading the message until he had it memorized, etched forever as a permanent fixture in his mind. A myriad of emotions surged through his immobilized body—elation, wonder, disbelief, skepticism, then anger. There were few words and many suggestions of interpretation. The part about Boston disturbed him and unseated a wagonload of doubts.

Resentment mounted steadily, and he clenched his fists. This was just like her, making demands. "Make me yours." The next part, "I love you," cut to the heart. He would not be taken in, however; she had said those words before, along with the explanation, "but not that way." And the final blow, "Boston suits fine." Of course it does, suits her high and mighty taste, her lofty ambitions.

Uncle Buck must have told her how the land lays. *She's after my money, my influence. Well, I won't settle for that. I don't have to. What a fool I've been.* He crumpled the paper and hurled it into a wastebasket. Grabbing for his coat, he strapped on his boots and threw open the latch.

A blast of wind snatched at his hat. He pulled it down tightly over his ears, set his shoulder against the tempest, and stomped off for home.

Before he reached his house on Beacon and Spruce, gigantic lacy flakes enveloped him, salting the shoulders of his dark jacket and covering his tracks. The Lord dusted Boston with its first snowfall of the season, but it fell unheralded by Thaddeas, who plodded on single-mindedly.

Stubborn pride settled in like the blanket of fog that so often fell over Boston, obscuring the vision of the city's occupants. It blinded him to the simple truth that Annabelle loved him. Unintelligible thoughts persisted. *She's after my inheritance. She does not want me, I'm like a brother to her—yet she will not release me. How can she be so cruel? I cannot live like this; I can take no more.*

These ideas, like whirring arrows, set him in flight, turning him in the direction of Mary Beth's house. That would clear his head; she was an intelligent woman who cared about him.

❧

Hours later, more to safeguard his affections than anything else, he made a hasty decision and heard himself utter the unrehearsed words, "I love you. Will you marry me?"

Mary Beth drew away, frightened at the intensity of his dark eyes. The coveted words tantalized her willing heart, but her spirit resisted. No trace of romance lit his face, only pain and desperation, unrelentless.

"Mary Beth?" He repeated her name.

"I do love you, Thad, but we must be sure."

"I'm sure. I've never been more determined in my life. Marry me," he urged.

"Yes." The words were soft as velvet and Thad pulled her almost roughly into his embrace.

Mary Beth's heart whispered encouragement. She genuinely loved this dark-haired beau, but sensed his love lacked full-ness. Oh, she could not doubt the passion pulsing through his sturdy body, but she wondered if it was enough to last a life-time.

❧

Thaddeas reflected on his day. What a long one it had been, starting with hours laboring over figures, then the unexpected telegram, and ending with his call on Mary Beth. She was a sweet young thing, innocent, self-sacrificing. He could not ask for a better wife or a prettier bride. After all, how long could one resist such a loving countenance, or those puppy eyes that had revealed infatuation for him from day one.

Then there was their families' joy when they shared their plans. Leon and Mother had been elated to learn he would stay on in Boston—at least for the time being. Who knew? Maybe some day Mary Beth and he would travel west. She'd make a good wife, and she would be willing to live wherever he decided.

Only one thing remained undone, and it would be the hardest, the most final. He swallowed the lump in his throat and scuffed across the room to rummage through the drawer of a small desk that set beneath his bedroom window.

Settling himself in its accompanying cane chair, with paper and pen posed, he stared at the delicate designs of snow and frost fast forming on the window and penned, "Dear Annabelle."

The words engraved upon his soul played over and over in his mind. "Make me yours. I love you. Boston suits me fine."

Thad's thoughts rambled, and he jumped up, threw a couple more logs into his fireplace, and paced the floor. Visions of copper curls glistening in the sun's light haunted him. Eyes green and full of fire, saucy cheeks, upturned nose, and tiny curved body all made up the creature who had commanded his heart for so long.

He collapsed on his bed, burying his dark face and heavy eyes into a comfortable feather-stuffed pillow, and willed Mary Beth's image into his mind. This would not do. He roused himself, returning to the task at hand, and yanked at the cane chair. It toppled over, and parchment paper floated helter-skelter about the floor. This was going to be a long night, but he would not go to bed until this letter was written. Then he could make a new beginning, one with Mary Beth.

fourteen

The first week's waiting was the hardest, expecting a telegram at any moment, scanning the horizon for the messenger boy, jumping out of her skin at every knock on the door. Even now, the second week, hope lingered. But if no word came by today, Annabelle resolved that Thad's reply would come via letter, taking four to six weeks—or maybe he would just show up at the door.

Annabelle reined Dusty in at the hitching post just outside Cooper's General Store. She knew, humanly speaking, there could be no letter yet; however, her heart raced as she made her way to the shop. Brushing the wrinkles out of her riding habit, she entered, her skirt swishing to the gentle movement of her hips.

It was enough to stop the heart of Andy Benson. Bart Barnes punched his buddy, "Look, across the street—Annabelle Larson!"

"I saw her." The young man continued to stare even after the massive plank door enveloped her, and she vanished from his sight. Without a word, Andy plodded toward the street in the direction of Cooper's General Store. Bart snickered and caught up with his friend.

The country lads paused a moment, then Andy pushed open the portal and they entered.

"Miss Larson, howdy." Both boys took off their hats and stood still for her inspection.

"Hello, Andy, Bart."

"You here to order some Christmas surprises?"

"In a way. Do you remember Luke Wheeler?"

76

"Yeah, sure! The preacher's son."

"Right. He works at an orphanage in Dayton and our family is going there for Christmas."

"To the orphanage? What for?"

Annabelle smiled. "That's the same question I asked. But Claire is so sentimental, she's convinced everyone to get involved, a charity project."

"Oh, I see. Yeah, Claire, she's got a soft spot, all right." When Annabelle gave Bart a strange look, he quickly added, "No harm intended, ma'am."

"None taken." Annabelle looped her arm through Andy's. They had known each other all of their lives, and though she knew he was sweet on her, she did not take him seriously, never considering her effect on him when she offered the slightest encouragement. She chattered as she led him toward the counter. "Mr. Cooper, I'm here to pick up the paper that we ordered."

"Sure, Annabelle, it's in."

She released Andy's arm and expressed delight at the package that Elias unwrapped: a stack of natural-colored parchment paper, cut into half sheets with holes punched in.

"Wow, you aren't going into teaching are you, Annabelle?" Andy asked.

Laughing, Annabelle denied it. "No. Claire is making diaries for the older girls at the orphanage. She thinks it might ease their pain to write down their feelings. Buck is getting the leather covers made, and Mattie is supplying the ribbon to bind the books together. Wouldn't mind having one myself."

"Maybe Claire will make you one for Christmas. I would if I knew how," Andy said quietly.

"Oh, Andy, you're so sweet," she said in one breath, and then, "Mr. Cooper, do we have any mail?" in the next.

"Jest a letter for the sheriff. Want it?"

"I'll take it." Annabelle placed it in the pocket of her riding skirt and fastened her coat as Elias carefully replaced the wrappings around the parchment paper and then offered her the bundle.

Andy grabbed for it and escorted the young woman outside, where he helped her mount.

"Have a good day," he called as Annabelle rode away. He watched her until she disappeared around a distant bend.

Bart spoke from a few feet away. "Why don't you call on her?"

"My timing is bad, I guess. I was all set to after Thaddeas left. Then that Harrison fellow showed up." Disgusted looks crossed both their faces, remembering the obnoxious intruder.

"I hear he's gone. No one's seen him for weeks."

"I know. Guess now there's no excuse, but I can't find the courage. She's just too elegant." Bart nodded his head in understanding.

᠀

"Look, Mattie, the paper was in!"

"Land sakes, let me see." They fingered the fragile paper wrappings, then Mattie said, "No! Go get Claire first."

"Where is she?"

"Out in the chicken coop scrounging for feathers. We still need more stuffing for those pillows."

"Even after all those feathers we got from Ben and the reverend?"

"Yes. Now, quickly, go get yer sister."

Annabelle flew out the door, letting it bang. She turned the corner where the giant hickory spread its bare limbs and stopped in her tracks. Snow! The first snowfall of the season in Beaver Creek. She looked skyward and wet flakes sprinkled her face. The flakes melted upon impact with the earth. She watched the process in fascination, each time expecting a trace of snow to remain upon the ground, disappointed when it vanished leaving only a damp circle.

"Claire! Claire!"

"In here." The call came as she suspected it would from the little shanty where the brown-winged fowl bunked. There was not a bird around, however, for when Claire had approached with gunny sack in hand they had fled for their lives. Stooped over with hair dangling in her face and spreading down her back, Claire diligently picked at each single feather that she spied, a tedious process. She did not look over her shoulder as she spoke. "Yes?"

"Your paper came."

"It did?" She yanked the strings on the mouth of the sack, swung it over her shoulder, and crouched to crawl through the small opening of the coop to greet her sister. "Great!"

"Missed one." Annabelle flicked a feather off Claire's cheek.

The girl scolded, "Hey, don't do that." She bent to pick up the solitary feather that had floated earthward landing on her boot, then noticed with pleasure, "It's snowing."

"Isn't it lovely? Look! It's sticking." The girls paused to take in its beauty, letting childhood memories flood over them. In a matter of minutes, the sky grew dark and the snow fell in heavy flurries.

They started toward the house, amazed that their world could turn white in such a short period of time. Claire glanced over her shoulder and pointed to some fresh markings in the now snow-covered ground behind them. "Tracks! Remember how we used to follow the animal trails after a newfallen snow?"

"Yes. But these are chicken tracks. And look where they lead. Right up those trees. They're roosting and waiting for us to clear out so they can return to their coop."

This brought Claire's thoughts back to the orphanage. "Hope it doesn't turn out to be a blizzard and ruin our trip to Dayton. Come on!" She hollered and rushed for the house.

"Mattie!" Claire called. "We won't have to cancel our trip for the snow, will we?"

Mattie frowned, fondling the unopened package containing Claire's paper. "I hope not. Depends on how deep it gets or icy. Nothin' we can do to change nature's doin's, so it won't do any good for ya ta worry 'bout it. Now, let's take a look at that paper."

While Claire opened the parcel for inspection, Mattie planned out loud. "We need to pick up the rest of the new comforters the church women are makin'. There's two more rag dolls ta make. The reverend and Mary's boys are doin' the boats for the smaller boys, Kate and Ben bought knives for the older boys, and the sheriff is gettin' the leather for your diaries."

"And I've enough feathers now for one more pillow." Claire and Mattie beamed with the satisfaction of accomplishment, but Annabelle's mind wandered.

She moved to the kitchen window and pushed the curtains aside to watch the winter storm. A chill tickled her spine, and she shuddered involuntarily. *I hope I hear from Thad before we leave for Dayton. Why doesn't he answer?*

fifteen

The weather cleared enough for travel and a few days before Christmas the entire entourage pulled into Dayton's fogged and frozen thoroughfare without much fuss from bystanders. Such sights, and ones many times more odd, frequently graced the city's cobblestones. But eyes gaped wide, those belonging to Annabelle and Claire, who hardly ever traveled, and then less frequently to a city.

They took in every aspect of the cluttered streets: the tall, groomed buildings, gloriously attired residents, and tattered beggars. Even as they watched from their wagon, a barefooted woman draped in a gray woolen shawl—partially covering her head as well as her back—stuck out a palm begging for a coin. "Jest need 'nuf for some firewood. My young uns are freezin' ta death," she called, exposing a nearly toothless mouth. Claire clapped her hand over her lips in horror as Buck tossed several coins toward the woman.

"Get out of the street!" yelled a small-framed man dressed in a suit and overcoat. "Go on. Be off with you." He waved his walking stick, but the woman paid no heed to the insults the man hurled, instead snatching the fallen money off the ground and stuffing it into her bosom. Claire crooked her neck to stare at the woman, who staggered along the street behind their wagon's trek.

Annabelle began to understand how sheltered they had lived. She feared Claire would become fainthearted, and reached a gloved hand toward her sister to utter some assurance when a raucous shout caught her attention. A clamor of unruly men gathered, encircling something as they hooted and shouted

81

obscenities. "I believe it's a brawl," Annabelle said, aghast.

Buck yelled back at the girls, "Don't be afraid. It's just a cockfight."

"Oh, how awful." Claire grimaced and covered her eyes.

"Look!" Annabelle nudged her sister. "The theater! Just like Dorie described." Couples mulled in front of a shop with a huge sign that announced the show time and performers. Annabelle strained to take it all in—the names on the billboard as well as what the ladies wore beneath their fur-trimmed cloaks.

As the wheels of the Larson wagon rumbled on, slipping into potholes, bouncing over rocks and pebbles, and clacking on the pavements, the jostled passengers soon realized they were leaving the heart of the city. Annabelle breathed deeply.

The smells were less pungent, the fog thinner. They must be going in the opposite direction of the river. But then, it was hard to tell as the waters came from all directions and seemed to network everywhere about them.

Claire gripped her sleeve, and Annabelle shifted to look where her sister pointed.

"That must be it!"

Annabelle recoiled, seeing her fears materialize in the form of a drab stone building sprawled out before them, bleak and uninviting. The place looked frightfully neglected and just like Annabelle had imagined the asylum. She was not the least surprised when children appeared, dressed in drab colors and ill-fitted garments.

"Oh, aren't they something?" Claire elbowed her sister, with wheels turning in her head. They were not given time to speculate as Buck instantly appeared to lift them to the ground, where they rubbed out their stiff muscles.

When Luke saw the group, the same ten, all-inclusive, from Thanksgiving Day, he was overcome with gratitude, hugging each in turn, and introducing them to those nearby, which soon included Catherine and Jesse Murdock.

"Land sakes, it's too cold to stand outside. Let's get the ladies indoors," Catherine urged. Mrs. Catherine Murdock took Annabelle by surprise. *Why she's beautiful,* she thought. In one solid look she memorized the woman from her pink oval face to her pointed, high-topped boots. Wearing an expression of rapture and serenity in perfect harmony, she flashed crystal blue eyes encircled in dark, long lashes. An abundance of yellow hair framed the woman's pleasant features supported by a lily-white neck. Her white-collared blouse was neatly tucked into a gray woolen skirt, which swished as she walked away.

"I'll help with the livestock," her equally exuberant husband offered. At his voice, deep and vibrant, Annabelle turned to see what kind of man this woman had married. She drew in a sharp breath, for he easily passed her inspection. *Yes, he would do.* Blushing, she moved to catch up with the other women and the band of children now entering the offensive habitation.

They were led into a long, rectangular-shaped room with many odds and ends of furniture scattered about. Some benches lined one wall, and Annabelle noticed a green settee and several padded chairs situated in a circle in front of a cavernous fireplace. A small table and chairs occupied either end, one with a checkerboard and checkers stacked from recent play.

"This is our parlor, such as it is." Mrs. Murdock waved her arms to include the expanse. "We all meet here in the evening to read or play games and visit. Please, sit there by the fire and warm yourselves, ladies."

"Are we done fer the 'day, Miss Catherine?" a child's voice questioned.

"Yes, dear." Mrs. Murdock smiled at the tow-headed boy who stood before her, shifting from one foot to the other. "This is Barney Forbes." Barney nodded. "Barnabus, why don't you assemble the other children, and when the men return we will make introductions all around." He agreed and rushed out of the room.

❧

That evening, supper was held in a huge dining hall with three very long tables. Mr. and Mrs. Murdock sat at one table with seven girls, Luke was in charge of six boys at another, and the visitors occupied the third. Mrs. Murdock and two older girls, Amity Jones and Brooke Forbes, both fourteen, served the dinner of stew, dumplings, and apple cobbler.

Afterwards, when the women visitors moved to help with the cleanup, a bubbly red-haired girl called Lacy spoke up, "No, ma'am . . . ladies. 'Tis our turn to do the dishes." She motioned to several boys and girls, aged seven to twelve, and they gathered the dishes.

"They take turns with various chores," Luke explained.

"Well, that may be," Mattie said, "but we want ta do our part while we're here."

"Very well." Mrs. Murdock seemed pleased. "But at least relax until tomorrow. I'm sure you're tired from your long journey."

They disassembled to the parlor, and Claire and Annabelle were soon encamped by a group of the older girls. One called Abigail spoke, "Brooke and I are sisters."

Brooke took up where her sister left off, "Hank, Barney, and Lonnie are our brothers." She pointed out two towheaded boys engaged in a game of marbles.

"Five of you?" Claire questioned.

"Yes, ma'am." Abigail went on, "We don't get many visitors."

"Please, don't call me ma'am," Claire said. "Why I'm not much older than you are, or your sister. Just call me Claire." Brooke shook her head. "No, that wouldn't be fitting. How about Miss Claire?"

"Good idea!" Claire patted her own sister's knee, "and this, then, is Miss Annabelle, my sister." Suddenly, Annabelle was tongue-tied for the first time in her life.

Across the room Kate rocked, singing lullabies to a shy, sleepy-eyed baby boy. Ben bounced the baby's three-year-old brother, Gabe, upon his knee. Gabe's round, freckled face looked up at him in wonder.

"Give Cody horsy ride, too?"

"I think Cody is falling asleep," Ben answered. Kate listened to Ben's deep, soft voice, soothing the tiny child. She marveled that the boy resembled the large man that held him.

Annabelle, touched with pity, listened to snatches of conversation. The children seemed content with so little. Some excited, and others leery, about Christmas Day gathered across the room as Luke explained what the special day, honoring the birth of a holy child, would hold, concluding with the promise of lots of surprises.

Long after the stars peeped out, the last of the orphans departed to retire for the evening in their simple rooms, where identical bunks lined the wall. Annabelle wondered if she would survive this ordeal. She felt exhausted.

sixteen

Annabelle concentrated on her task of braiding Lacy Gray's unmanageable hair.

"Your hair's the same as mine," Lacy stated.

Annabelle considered the comparison. "I never liked it when folks said my hair was red—it would make me fighting mad."

"I know," the nine-year-old said softly.

"I'd say, nope, it's auburn, or copper-colored, or my favorite, cinnamon fluff."

"Cinnamon fluff?" The little girl wrinkled her nose, then remarked, "I like that."

"Or cinnamon sticks, since yours is neatly braided."

Lacy giggled.

"Now, quit squirming. We need to hurry. After all, it's Christmas morning."

◆

Annabelle observed those crowded together to hear Luke read the Christmas story. Some reclined in chairs, others sprawled on the threadbare carpet. Excitement danced in the children's eyes. They looked forward to the times Luke read to them from his Bible, for his voice was animated and his large hands expressive. Because it was Christmas, the air was charged with the element of the unexpected.

Between pokes from the tiny fingers of Lacy and her sisters, who competed for her attention, Annabelle watched James and Frank roughhouse playfully with some of the boys who were as noisy as an Indian war party. Barney's head, as always, popped up from the center of the scuffle.

Cody and Gabe cuddled in the laps of Ben and Kate while

Claire sat shoulder to shoulder between two older girls. Luke shook hands with a visitor, a burly blacksmith named Luther Woods, but when he came to Woods' indentured servant, Adam Parks, Luke gave the boy an emotional bear hug.

Reverend William Hamer, the Presbyterian preacher under whom Luke served, and his family were present. The dark-haired clergyman wore a look of approval.

At last, Luke settled in a chair, opened his worn Bible, and began. Captivated, Annabelle realized Luke recited many portions from memory.

"'And there were shepherds living out in the fields nearby, keeping watch over their flocks at night. An angel of the Lord appeared to them, and the glory of the Lord shone around them, and they were terrified. But the angel said to them, "Do not be afraid. I bring you good news of great joy that will be for all the people. Today in the town of David a Savior has been born to you; he is Christ the Lord. This will be a sign to you: You will find a baby wrapped in cloths and lying in a manger (Luke 2:8-12).'""

He paused, letting the leather-bound black book rest on his lap. Luke knew there would be questions, like always, and waited patiently for the words to soak into the little sponges camped about him.

"Did he have a ma and pa? The baby?"

Luke studied Barney intently and answered, "Yes. Mary was His ma and Joseph was His pa. But, He was also the son of God."

"Whew!" Barney exclaimed. "That's somethin'."

Luke continued, "God sent His Son to be the Savior of the world. He let Him come as a baby, so that He might be our Savior."

"Did God leave Him in the manger just like our folks left us outside the livery stable?" Lacy asked with astonishment.

The room grew quiet and Luke cleared his throat. The Grays

had abandoned their daughters when they passed through
Dayton six months earlier, entrusting Lacy at age nine to care
for her two younger sisters. The girls were found huddled
together outside a livery stable. Lacy had explained there were
eleven children in all, and her pa always complained that he
had too many mouths to feed. Luke figured they needed the
older ones to do the work, and the youngest ones had not been
deserted solely because they were male.

"I'm sure it was hard for God to send His Son, and also hard
for your folks to leave you girls. They knew that they didn't
have enough food and money to care for you. I know it's diffi-
cult to understand. But we love you very much." Luke held out
his arms and the three little girls scooted into them.

"What about Santa Claus?" Lonnie asked. There were snick-
ers around the room from the older children.

Luke tactfully avoided the question and asked, "What about
presents? Are we ready to open gifts?" The room buzzed with
excitement. "All right. James and Frank, would you like to
pass out the packages?" Names had been placed on the gifts
and the two young men carefully matched them to the proper
recipients.

ra

Later the girls, tucked in their rooms for the night, cuddled
new rag dolls and cherished diaries. The boys were content
with their boats and knives, and they all snuggled under new
comforters and rested their weary heads on feather pillows.

The exhausting day wound to a close with the adults gathered in front of the parlor fire, discussing the day's events.

"It didn't even snow for Christmas," Annabelle murmured
as the heat of the flame licked her cheeks.

"But it was the best Christmas I ever had," Claire remarked.
"And snow might have kept us from coming."

"Or stranded us, here at Dayton," Annabelle added.

"I wish I could stay and help. Can I, Luke?" Claire's face

showed her eagerness.

"We could use the extra help."

"I jest don't know; you're so young." Mattie looked to Buck for support—some reason why their daughter could not remain at the orphanage—but he remained quiet, only responding by placing his arm around his wife and squeezing.

Noting Mattie's strong objection, Luke explained with gentleness, "You cannot stay this time, Claire, without your belongings or Mattie's blessing. Give your folks some time to decide; pray about it. Then, if you choose to help, we will be glad to have you."

Claire nodded in resignation, and relief washed over Mattie.

Ben saw his opportunity and jumped in, "Luke, tell us how we can adopt Gabe and Cody."

Luke's eyes sparkled at Ben's request and he glanced at Jesse Murdock across the room, who replied, "If you want to make it legal and give them your name, papers need to be drawn up. We're mighty grateful that you want them. You're fine folks and would make the boys good parents."

"Thank you." Kate addressed the Murdocks anxiously. "How long would it take? We need to leave tomorrow."

"It would be better if we waited, dear." Ben spoke softly to his wife. "We can return for them."

Jesse agreed. "Probably be best for all of the children to have time to prepare them. It's always a loss to the others when some leave. They take it hard."

As Annabelle listened, her stomach churned with feelings of guilt and grief—a sensation that was now a constant companion. It had first appeared after Thad's proposal and grew more intense when Thaddeas moved to Boston. The same pain tormented her after Charles' note and taunted her on a regular basis since she realized she loved Thad. Its agitation provided a steady reminder of her unanswered telegram.

Now, though, its cause was the sorrow she felt for the children, combined with the knowledge that she was not like Claire. She could never go into ministry. She just wanted to flee, get as far away from here as fast as she could. The miserable feeling boiled her insides.

ᔥ

"Claire, you asleep?" Annabelle whispered to the girl who lay beside her.

"No. What is it?"

"This place upsets me. I feel like I got the jitters."

"Me too. I can't stand not being able to help. I want to come back more than anything in the world. It means everything to me."

"I can see it's a good thing. They need contributions and support, but it hurts too much to be around them. How could you cope?"

"Well, there's pain all right, but it won't go away just because we walk away from here. And I have peace with God that this is a ministry I'm supposed to do."

"If it is, Mattie and Buck have to let you come. But I'd miss you terribly. The thought of it makes me feel even worse. I keep losing everyone I love."

"Do you mean Charles?"

"No. He hurt my pride but I never loved him."

"Thaddeas?"

"Yes. I miss him so much sometimes I think I can't bear it."

"Oh, Annabelle, I'm sorry."

"There's nothing that can be done about it. We'd better get some sleep."

"I'll pray for you."

"Thanks."

"Good night."

seventeen

At Tucker House a few weeks later, Annabelle listened carefully as her sister, Kate, explained.

"I'm mixed up. I thought adopting Cody and Gabe would be the best thing on earth, but instead it's set my world spinning."

"What do you mean, Kate?"

"At first it was exciting, planning what needed to be done for their arrival. The loft had to be cleaned. The place had become a storage post. Ben said he'd make two beds and a stand for it. We needed sheets, comforters, pillows, and clothes for the boys." Her voice trailed off at this point and she lapsed into a state of reflection.

"You look exhausted. Perhaps you're trying to do too much."

"We've barely scratched the surface and it's driving a wedge between Ben and me."

Annabelle's mouth flew open of its own accord, in an unflattering gesture, at this piece of information. "Why? Doesn't Ben want the children?"

Kate pulled a hanky out of her apron pocket and dabbed at her eyes. "I thought so. Maybe he just wanted them for me." Then she said sarcastically, "The way he's sulking and moping, I can't believe he's trying to please me. I don't know what's wrong with him."

Annabelle did not know what to make of this muddled explanation. Kate and Ben were the perfect couple, and Kate always had everything under control. She patted her sister's hand and listened.

"Ben makes promises that he doesn't keep." She continued

between sobs. "He said he'd make those beds and he hasn't even begun."

"Perhaps he's just been busy."

"Yes, he has. Doing stuff for other people. He spent a couple days helping his father mend fences. He and Jude Miller put up a new outhouse, and he even spent a day fishing with Frank and James. Real important things!"

"It sounds to me like you should be the one that is cross. Why is Ben sulking?" Annabelle became angry at her brother-in-law.

"I don't know. But he's barely speaking to me. I've been doing what I can. Cleaned the loft until it sparkled. Took the wagon to town myself for material and then stayed up all hours of the night knotting those comforters," she sighed, "and sewing little trousers."

Kate remembered the first night she had been up late. Ben had been cheerful enough, even playful. She had to get quite stern with him before he had left her alone to work on them. Finally, he had gone to bed.

She tried to remember when his ill temper had started, but she could not. She was so engrossed in her tasks, the days and nights all ran together. Finally Ben had understood the importance of the matter and had quit pestering her each night.

Then he started in with his little demands. There had been a few arguments about making their little beds, and now this dreaded silence—each going about their own duties. She shrugged her shoulders; she just could not remember anything she had done to offend him nor could she understand why he was dragging his feet about the children.

"I'm afraid to ask him when he plans to get to the beds. He'll probably bite my head off."

"You poor thing," Annabelle murmured.

"When he finds out I came over today he might be upset." Kate looked sheepish. "I didn't tell him I was coming."

"I'm sorry Mattie wasn't here. She would know exactly what to tell you. The sheriff and her have their squabbles."

"They do?"

"Yes." Annabelle nodded. "Of course, they don't last long."

This information encouraged Kate, who had not known if such arguments were normal or irregular. She only knew they upset her.

A thought suddenly hit her, *Neither Ben nor I had a set of parents to watch as children. There is so much to learn about marriage.* On its heels came another thought, *Quit thinking about yourself, try to understand Ben.* Next came a great desire to go home and spend some time alone with God. "Well, I'd best be getting home now. I feel much better, really I do."

≈

After the dust from Kate's wagon settled, Annabelle stood on the front steps of Tucker House reflecting over the things Kate had said. *Men!* She thought of her love telegram that continued to go unanswered. *Is that what Thaddeas is doing to me . . . giving me the silent treatment?* She wondered if he was trying to get even with her, to prove something. It was not like him to play games, and he did not leave Ohio angry with her. *Could he have grown bitter in such a short time?*

≈

Two days later, Mattie received a caller. This one found her at home and alone. She patted her honey-colored hair, with nimble fingers tucking strands of unruly pieces into place in the twist where they belonged, and called, "Comin'."

The caller heard her voice and stiffened, waiting for the door to open. When it did, Mattie gasped and stared for a long time.

Finally the man spoke, "Hello, Mattie." His voice was familiar, though deeper and edged with tremor.

She flushed. "Hello, Wade."

"May I come in?"

Mattie looked over her shoulder at the vacant house and many thoughts raced through her mind. *What does he want? It isn't fittin' with Buck not here.* "I-I don't know . . ."

"I realize I've got no right to ask. But I only want to talk. Please."

Again she hesitated, "I don't think it would be proper . . ."

Wade pulled an envelope from the inside of his military jacket and held it in full view. "I have a letter from your folks." Mattie's full attention riveted to the document in his fist. The hook sufficiently planted, he returned the envelope to his pocket and waited.

This was unexpected news and Mattie placed her hand across her fluttering heart. "All right," she said, "come on in."

The six-foot man followed her into the sitting room, taking in the surroundings. The smell of lavender trailed behind the straight, slim backside of the woman he had once loved. The realization that she was more beautiful than he had remembered shook him.

While obsessed to know all about her—every detail of the last twenty-three years—he perceived the need to proceed cautiously. The lieutenant noted Mattie's strength, the courageous glint in her eyes, and the firm set of her mouth. Every movement signified stubborn resistance to his presence.

When they were seated, stiff as two starched shirts, Mattie gave him an icy stare. She saw flashes of his youth but mostly a commanding lieutenant, unrecognizable. His eyes though were soft pools, and lines of worry grooved his temple.

"Mattie. I know I have acted dishonorably. May I explain?"

"It's not necessary," she snapped.

"But I want to."

"What good can come of it? That's all in the past."

"It needs to be righted."

"How can it be?"

He smiled. "You're a strong woman, Mattie."

"I had to be."

"I was wrong to do what I did. I was young and afraid of the preacher, your father." Mattie's eyes glistened with astonishment. She understood fear of the tyrant. "But that is no excuse," Wade continued. "To leave you to face the bully alone was abominable."

The lieutenant unconsciously crushed the hat on his lap, then ran his fingers through his saddle-brown hair. "I joined the cavalry. When my term expired, I returned home, expecting to take up my responsibilities, but you had vanished. I went to visit your father."

Mattie smiled in spite of herself, imagining what that scene had been like. "You must have been courageous," she said, bitterness tainting her voice.

"He disowned you, and wouldn't give me any information, so I joined up for another hitch. After the Indian raid, your parents were overcome with grief. That was when I learned that you'd gone to Big Bottom to live with your sister, Elizabeth . . . and our baby. But they said you were all killed."

He continued, "I married and had a son." Mattie's brows arched, but still she said nothing. "My son is fourteen, and my wife, Hannah, died a couple years back." Sorrow laced his voice, and Mattie discovered she felt some compassion for the man.

Wade noticed her countenance softening and added with more enthusiasm, "I got stationed at Fort Wayne and made trips along this territory, where I heard of Tucker House and Mattie Tucker. It seemed a miracle, and I just had to know if it was really you!"

Mattie replied, her voice low and reflective, "All these years, I never knew what happened to ya. Then Buck, my husband, ran across you at the Golden Lamb. He mentioned your name 'pon his return."

"Does he know about us?"

"Yes. He knows it all."

"I guess my purpose in coming is twofold." The brown-eyed

officer took a gulp of courage. "I come to ask for your forgiveness and to see if our child is alive."

"With the Lord's help, I'll forgive you."

Wade Brooks bestowed Mattie with a generous smile. "Thank you." He hesitated to press her. He had come so far with this woman who sat so straight yet looked so vulnerable, but he ventured. "And our child?"

"I raised three daughters, orphans from the Indian raid, that is all."

"I know. Is one of them our daughter?" Mattie stared at him stubbornly, refusing to reply. "One is the right age," he continued.

Mattie rose. "You have no right to ask. Anyway, what's done is done. What's past is past. Buck wouldn't like ya bein' here." She pointed to the door. "You really must leave now, lieutenant."

"Very well, Mattie. I see you are distressed. However, it's important for me to know if I have a daughter." He paused to emphasize his point. "My work takes me through these parts frequently. I will let you think about what we have discussed and stop another time."

"Please, don't. I've had a lonely life, but I'm happy now. I don't need you turnin' over old stones; just stirs up trouble."

"I'm sorry you see it that way, Mattie. I just want to make things right." His next words stuck like tree sap. "If I have a daughter, then I owe it to her."

As Wade Brooks turned to go, he remembered the letter from her folks. "Here, Mattie. And think about it. I know you'll do the right thing and see me again. Good-bye."

After he left, Mattie stared at the envelope that lay on her lap. Finally, she tore it open.

Dear Mattie,
We took you for dead, but Wade claims you are alive.

I've made many mistakes in my lifetime, but what I did to you was the worst. Please forgive me. Your mother longs to hear from you.

Your Pa,
Reverend Tucker

Mattie wept bitterly until her tears were spent. Then she prayed. "Oh, Lord, I cannot forgive them on my own. Can you help me?"

eighteen

Annabelle's breast felt as if it caged a wild bird. She sought to still the fluttering wings beating against her bosom by seeking refuge at a favorite spot. Brushing the snow off the bench with mittened hands, she seated herself where the sun's warming rays could be felt beneath the bare-branched hickory tree, a comfortable haven, alone. Her disappointment and anxiety over the past six weeks since she had sent that telegram had taken a toll on her.

She realized by now that Thaddeas was not overjoyed by her message or he would have sent an immediate reply. The padded letter she now held in her hands contained his answer, yet she hesitated to read its contents.

Remembering the night she had sat under this same tree with Thad, she pulled off her mittens and placed them on the bench. It was the night before he had left for Boston, and he had offered marriage. How she wished she could take her answer back, could be in Boston with him today.

Just then a rabbit scampered across the yard—within a few yards of her. Upon the scent of danger, it froze like a statue, except for the tiny, twitching nose. Annabelle murmured to the diversion, "Are you as scared as I am, little fellow?"

When her voice pricked the air, the long ears shot skyward, and in a cotton flurry he hopped away, the giant feet zigzagging a trail in the snow-covered ground. "I guess you are," she sighed. "Well, I can't run away like you."

She carefully opened the letter, smoothing out the sheets of paper on her lap. Picking up the first page, she read:

Dear Annabelle,

I received your telegram today and decided to write a letter. My heart is full, and there is too much to say in a telegram. I have loved you for a very long time, but I believe that our ambitions are far too different for us to make a life together.

Annabelle's hands trembled and large tears glistened on her cheeks. She instinctively knew her world was falling apart, but she continued to read.

Your ambitions are lofty ones, dreams of gold, pearls, balls, and parties.

Fleeting thoughts of Charles Harrison and the hopes she had harbored at that time flashed before her eyes. She remembered her haughty attitude with Thaddeas and recalled her vain words. She did not know when, but those ambitions had been replaced with hurt, doubts, emptiness, and the all-encompassing loneliness that haunted her since Thad left.

My dreams include hard work and adventure, living my life for Jesus Christ, and following His direction. I am looking for a woman who will love me as much as I love her, be willing to live in a shack or a castle—a woman filled with passion and compassion—who would not be afraid to dirty her hands for any task set before her.

A hope quivered in her breast. Yes, she could be that woman. She would show him, let him know that she had changed.

I believe that I have been patient with you, nurturing in our relationship, careful not to force myself or my

Lord upon you. You turned my proposals down so em-
phatically, I can only believe that it is not possible that
you love me.

"Poor Thad. Oh, I must let him know that I really do
love him."

You must, therefore, love my friendship, my money,
my influence, or my Boston. But I know you cannot truly
love me.

But I do, Annabelle's heart screamed. *I do!* Frantically she
read on.

Since coming to Boston, I have met a woman who has
all of the qualifications I am looking for in a wife. Her
name is Mary Beth Edwards. Her love for me is unself-
ish and pure. I have asked her to be my wife and she has
accepted.

Annabelle felt the shock of Thad's declaration pulse like a
wave through every part of her being, leaving her paralyzed as
it inched along. When it reached her feet, it seemed that her
life's force drained onto the frozen ground, leaving her a lonely
shell of a person. She did not know how long she sat there in
denial and grief.

Finally, she realized several sheets of paper remained. *What*
is this? Endless praises of his betrothed? Then an urgency
possessed her to know more about this woman who had stolen
Thaddeas from her. Angry, she gripped the letter and read on.

I am sure that it will not take you long to set your
affections upon some other young man. Many will be as
spellbound as I was. I will continue to pray for you, that
you will come to know the Lord Jesus Christ, and that

*you will find a life that is fulfilling. I remain affection-
ately yours,*

> *Your cousin,*
> *Thaddeas*

*P.S. I have enclosed a letter for Uncle Buck and would
appreciate it if you would see that he gets it.*

"That's it? That's all? He is dismissing me. He cannot do
this! I won't stand for it! The rest of this is a letter—for Buck.
This cannot be happening. He said he would always be there
for me."

"Annabelle!"

She saw Claire standing on the steps, but the sound of her
sister's voice seemed miles away.

"Come in for supper!"

The bewildered young woman waved her letter-stuffed hand
in the air, acknowledging Claire's request. How could she face
the others? In a whirl of confusion she gathered up her skirts
and ran to the house, wherein she flew through the kitchen
and clamored up the steps to her room.

"What on earth?" Mattie dropped the dishcloth she held and
chased up after her. When she entered Annabelle's room, she
rushed to the sobbing girl. "Child, what is wrong?"

Annabelle thrust Thad's letter into Mattie's hand. "Here.
Read it for yourself. Thaddeas is engaged," and she burst into
another fit of tears. Mattie drew the young woman into her
arms and held her tightly. "Oh darlin', I'm so sorry. I know
how it must hurt ya."

ૐ

Six weeks had passed since Thaddeas had written Annabelle.
Daily, the young man thrust his energy into his work at the
leather shop, where his relationship with his brother, Leon,
was renewed. His evenings found him with his mother or his
affianced, Mary Beth.

Christmas came and went, a pleasant time when Thaddeas and Mary Beth discussed likes and dislikes and discovered they had numerous things in common. In planning their future, Mary Beth professed undying love and loyalty and a desire to follow Thad wherever he might go. The sensitive creature knew exactly when to tease and flirt, lassoing Thaddeas with love and attention, tightening the knot with pleasant words and passing days.

Just occasionally, he questioned his own motives. Once when he had gazed into her eyes, green fiery ones glared back instead of the gentle turquoise ones Mary Beth possessed, and he cursed himself for thinking of another but his beloved.

Another time, he snapped back at her when she succumbed without a thought to one of his plans. "Woman," he had said. "Don't be afraid to have an opinion of your own. A little pluck is good for the soul." She had cried, making him feel like a beast. Realizing he had compared her unjustly to Annabelle, he determined to make her happy, love her more devotedly.

On this January day, however, his troubles were not romantically inclined but focused on a pressing dilemma.

"Perhaps we should dip into our investments and buy a warehouse to store goods without cost, and later resell the property," Amelia Larson suggested to her two sons.

"I think we should wait it out," Leon urged. "Jefferson cannot let this thing go on for any length of time."

"When I first read the headlines back in December of this Embargo Act, I knew it would be trouble." Thaddeas hit his fist against his thigh in protest of the disturbing bill Congress had passed under Jefferson's persuasion. "Why, England and France are laughing at us—especially England, she's getting richer by the day.

"Last year alone the United States exported eight thousand boots and one hundred twenty thousand shoes. The industry cannot handle this restraint. While the shoes pile up in warehouses, we cannot move our leather."

Amelia questioned her son, "Is there a domestic product that could use our leather, some item we have overlooked? Does it all have to go to shoes, boots, harnesses, and saddles?"

"None that we can think of at the present, Mother." Leon shook his head thoughtfully.

"I was just going to give our workers a raise. They deserve more than fifteen shillings a week," Thaddeas complained. "Now I'm afraid we'll have to lay some off instead. We'll keep on the apprenticeships; they are cheap and will provide good labor when the seas open up again. But I hate to put people out of a job when they have been faithful."

"We could lay off Peterson. He's a troublemaker, anyway."

"Yes, I suppose he shall be the first to go," Thaddeas agreed. "I guess our most pressing question is whether we can wait any longer before we take some action."

"I think we should wait," Leon offered.

"I am willing," Amelia agreed.

Thaddeas sighed. "All right." Then he rose to leave. "I'll be in my room until supper, if I'm needed." He climbed the spiral staircase, gliding his hand along the smooth oak banister. Perfectly shined boots stepped off the distance of the long hallway and took him to his large, masculine-looking room. When he opened the door, a crackling fire welcomed him. The scent of rose water filled the air to remind him the maid had prepared a basin to freshen for supper.

He stared at the large painting above his four-poster bed. The western setting, usually so soothing, depressed him today. Purple mountains loomed, calling his name. The smiling cowboys mocked him as they herded mangy cattle with lassos high overhead and prairie grass underfoot.

He dropped to a kneeling position on the oval rug that warmed the floor at the side of the bed. His forehead pounded as if the cattle in the painting stampeded across his head, and he poured out his troubled heart to God.

nineteen

In the days following the announcement of Thad's engagement to Mary Beth, Annabelle went through many stages of
coping with her grief. One of her first reactions—anger—she
vented upon Andy Benson when he finally mustered up enough
courage to call one Sunday afternoon.

"Evenin', Miss Annabelle."

Annabelle watched the young man shuffle from one foot to
the other and quickly grew impatient with the tongue-tied
intruder.

"Yes?" She tapped her booted foot as if counting off the seconds he was allotted before she shut the door.

"'Tis a cold day, isn't it?" he ventured.

"Perhaps you'd better state your intentions then?"

"Ma'am?"

"What can I do for you, Andy?"

"Well, I thought I'd . . . that is . . . I'd come callin'."

"What?" Annabelle frowned. "Do you want to see Claire?"

"No, ma'am. I came to see you, Miss Annabelle."

"That's impossible! Why should you call on me?"

She then dismissed him so coldly that Mattie, who had overheard the end of the conversation, insisted she ride Dusty to
his farm to apologize. Reluctantly, Annabelle did. She expressed
regrets for her rude behavior in all meekness, but Andy—much
impressed with her sour temperament—vowed he would never
call upon her again, which suited Annabelle fine.

Days on end of melancholy and listless existence led Annabelle
toward introspection, followed by extended periods of weeping.
This drove Claire wild. She could not stand to hear the wretched
sobs penetrating the wall between their dark rooms.

She tried to comfort her older sibling and received tongue lashings in return. Still, she persevered. At just such a time, she approached Annabelle with an idea. "I know just the thing for you," Claire said.

"And what is that?" The tone of Annabelle's voice dripped of acidity.

"Why don't you come with me to work at the orphanage? You can get your mind off Thaddeas by helping the children. A city like Dayton is bound to have many diversions."

"You don't even have permission to go to the orphanage."

"I know. But with your persuasion, Mattie and Buck would give in."

This challenge became a tiny bubble of a catalyst that gradually propelled Annabelle out of her phase of lethargy. She considered. "You think so?"

2a

After lengthy discoursing and debates, Buck and Mattie agreed to allow the girls to move to Dayton. Buck, who never had been against the idea, supported Mattie as best he could, gently assuring his wife that it was the right decision.

He had to go easy with her these days as she was taut as a fiddle. The lieutenant had asked questions around town, then paid her another call, and she was not handling it well. Buck had been present when the lieutenant dropped by, an awkward situation for all of them.

When Brooks left, the Larsons got into a heated debate, for Buck believed Mattie was dead wrong to withhold information from Wade Brooks about his daughter. However, she remained steadfast about it and there was nothing he could do to bend her thinking. It was her decision to make.

Though Mattie was a good woman who usually channeled her stubbornness in a constructive manner, Buck knew she was hard to come up against head on. He learned fast that patient nudging and gentle counsel went further in changing her mind than butting heads like a couple of mountain goats.

After informing the girls that they were allowed to help at the orphanage, telegrams ripped like lightning between Beaver Creek and Dayton. The girls sent the first message:

> Luke,
> Have permission. Desire to come help at orphanage.
> Annabelle and Claire

Luke replied:

> Annabelle and Claire,
> All is set. I will come for you. Arrival February 10.
> Luke

❧

Ben Wheeler held a different telegram in his hand that pricked like a sliver of wood from his corral and needed to be dealt with immediately. He knew if he waited until evening it would fester all day long, so he headed for the house to find his wife. The telegram addressed the issue that had turned his household upside down.

"Kate."

"In here." Kate came out of their bedroom, wondering what Ben wanted. She had not heard him return from his ride into town. No small talk had been exchanged between the two lately, so she knew something important was afoot if he called her name now.

In the last several weeks life had grown tenser by the minute at the old Potter place, with Ben expelling a great amount of energy on his chores, which he did in silence. Meals had turned into dismal affairs, and most often, afterwards, Ben would go to the barn to check on the animals while Kate burst into a fit of tears. She continued to work on the clothes for Gabe and Cody—the comforters now complete—until Ben fell asleep each night, then she dropped wearily onto the far edge of the bed they shared.

The loft remained empty, and the small beds and table Ben had agreed to make were never discussed. Both Ben and Kate spent time in prayer about the issue. Each, at different times, came to the verge of confession or forgiveness of their spouse, when a swell of pride or new accusations hindered the reconciliation.

Just this morning, when Ben rode away with the dust licking at his heels, Kate had fled to her room, dropped to her knees, and begged God to intervene.

Now Ben hung his coat on the peg behind the door and removed his hat. "Please sit down, Kate." She obeyed, fidgeting with her hands in her lap. Finding himself mute, Ben handed her the telegram. "Here."

Kate read the words that her husband had memorized.

> *Ben and Kate,*
> *Arriving February 10, to escort Larson girls to Dayton. Could bring adoption papers and boys. Please advise.*
> > *Luke.*

"What does this mean, to escort Larson girls?"

"I stopped in on the way home. Annabelle and Claire are both going to the orphanage for awhile to help out."

"What! Why, I can't believe Annabelle would do this. She usually tells me everything."

"You haven't been the most sociable lately."

Kate's face burned at the insult, and tears stung her eyes. She did not reply. After a loaded silence, Ben continued.

"What answer should I give Luke?"

"No. Tell him no." Kate spat out the words. She got up from her seat and ran across the room to their bedroom, slamming the door behind her and flinging herself across the bed.

Ben instantly wished he had bitten his tongue instead of insulting Kate. He hated his behavior of the last several weeks, yet continued in the same destructive pattern, powerless to change it. Even with nonresistance a part of his lifestyle, he would rather take blows from any man than suffer the rejection he had been experiencing from his young wife. He found himself wondering if she had only married him to have children. Not able to provide her with them, she now cast him aside like a rusty nail.

Regardless of the truth, he could not go on this way, with life crashing in all around him. He crossed the room to their closed bedroom door and lifted his fist to knock, but he could not. What would he say? He lowered it again. *Lord*, he prayed, *give me the words to say*. Then he gently rapped on the door. "Kate?"

"Go away."

"I'm sorry. May I come in?"

"No."

"Please." This time there was no reply, so he eased the door open and lowered himself onto the bed beside his wife. Her whimpers tore at his heart and he pulled her into an embrace; they clung to each other. The physical touch began to dissolve the wall of pride and misunderstanding that stood between them. Apologies poured out.

"I'm sorry, Darling."

"What have I done to make you so angry?" Kate moaned.

"I am not angry, just hurt. I feel like you don't want me around anymore."

"Why would you feel that way?"

"You've turned me out, Kate." He did not want to make her angrier, and carefully worded his thoughts. "Since we've been married, our evenings were always special. Lately, you're preoccupied." She stared at him, trying to comprehend. "That isn't all. I wondered if once we got Cody and Gabe, you'd even share my bed anymore."

Like a shooting star, understanding dawned for Kate. "Oh, Ben, I'm so sorry. I didn't realize what I was doing. I love you more than anything. I've been so lonely without you, and so foolish to let things go on like they have, each of us going our separate ways."

Realizing there was a great deal that they did not understand about each other or about nurturing a marital relationship, Ben pulled his Bible off the nearby nightstand.

"Want to know what the Lord's been saying to me? Of course, I was too mule-headed to listen."

"All right."

"Here it is, Ephesians 4:26, 'Do not let the sun go down while you are still angry.' I vow this will never happen again in our household, if we have to stay up all night talking."

"I didn't listen to the Lord either. I'm so sorry."

Recognizing the fragile state of their emotions, they agreed to put off the adoption for a while, devoting time to each other and their relationship. Thus, Luke was much surprised when he received their telegram which read,

> *Luke,*
> *Not ready to adopt at this time. Will discuss on your visit.*
>
> *Ben*

twenty

February tenth, one month after Annabelle had received Thad's letter of dismissal, she found herself reasonably settled in her new surroundings. Her strenuous days proved to be anything but routine for they centered around thirteen energetic children.

The first week passed, a killer. Every part of her body ached from bending, lifting, toting. With the endless number of chores, Annabelle could not imagine how Luke and the Murdocks had gotten along before she and Claire had come to help. But the ceaseless duties, rather than taxing her, provided a numbing effect, and she could finally get her mind off her problems.

In a short while, these new activities became an integral part of her existence, and Beaver Creek seemed like part of a distant dream. This was reality—up at dawn, washing, ironing, mending, baking, and tending the children.

She became especially attached to her young red-headed clone, Lacy Gray. Taking Lacy underfoot meant caring for Lacy's tiny sisters, as well. Ever since their parents had deserted them, they tagged along behind Lacy like baby chicks following a mother quail.

Annabelle felt sorry for the little girl because there were no other girls her age to play with, only boys. Not the tomboy type, Lacy oftentimes felt left out.

❧

Sunday was a day they all looked forward to. Sometimes they attended the Reverend Hamer's Presbyterian church in Dayton, but most often, Luke preached the Sunday morning meeting in the huge parlor. In the afternoon, following dinner, they relaxed or participated in a special fun activity.

On this particular Sunday, they planned to go sledding behind the orphanage on the hills that looked like the rumps of sleepy bears. The children heard the fable told each winter—how all the polar bears from Antarctica come to this particular spot to rest on their tummies and hibernate for the winter. Of course, they knew this could not be true for the children often tromped and explored these snow-covered hills, within walking distance.

Today the children, anxious to occupy the slopes again, listened to Luke finish his sermon. "Therefore, children, remember that God loves you in a very special way. Psalm 68:5 says, 'A father to the fatherless, a defender of widows, is God in his holy dwelling.' This God who created the universe knows everything about each one of you. He is the same God who made the snow."

This caught the children's attention, and Luke set a beautiful picture before them of a magnificent God. "Job says in chapter thirty seven, verses five and six, 'He does great things beyond our understanding. He says to the snow, "Fall on the earth," and to the rain shower, "Be a mighty downpour."'" And this all-powerful God wants to be your Father. He wants you to come to Him with all your cares. Pray to him every day, bringing to His attention all of the things you are doing, your accomplishments, and your needs. He promises to be there for you.

"Heavenly Father," he prayed, "thank You for creating an ice palace for us, complete with heaps of snow and slick hills that make sleds go fast. Thank You for Your love."

After the "amen", children's bodies scurried this way and that, checking their duties on the blackboard that hung on the wall between the dining room and kitchen. Dishes and utensils appeared. Youngsters carried bowls and glasses, and performed the various errands needed to serve the Sunday meal.

Afterwards, just as many chipped in for cleanup, eager to be off to explore the snowy hills.

Annabelle walked with Lacy and pulled Neda and Missy on the sled, leaving wiggly grooves that blended in with the tracks made by the other four sleds, thirteen children, and five grown-ups. Annabelle glanced at Claire and thought that life at the orphanage agreed with her. She looked a vision of health. Her cheeks glowed and eyes sparkled as she chattered with those grouped about her.

Puffs of steam encircled them and drifted skyward as they huffed their way uphill to the top of the nearest bluff. The hill was not high but steep, and provided an excellent road course for the outing. When the sleds were lined up on the ridge and loaded with willing bodies, Luke and Jesse pushed them off. Giggles from the spectators nearly drowned out the squeals of the riders. After they reached the bottom, the youngsters headed uphill with sleds pulled behind them to give the next child a turn.

All the children had taken several spins before Luke suggested that Annabelle and Claire take a turn. Side by side they eyed each other, then Luke said, "Ready," and they were off. The wind slapped Annabelle's face soundly, sucking out her breath, spraying snow all the while, and the trees sped by like arrows. Her stomach lurched, then hung in her chest until the sled finally glided to a smooth landing. She sat still a moment while a rush coursed through her veins, settling in her stomach, which returned to its proper place. Then she climbed off as quickly as her bundled body could manage. When she saw her sister's teary eyes and red nose, she called, "Wasn't that great?"

"Wonderful!"

Joyously they made their ascent and turned over their wooden fliers to those next in line.

Annabelle laughed at Lacy's face, screwed up into a frown

because she had to double up with ten-year-old Hank Forbes. When Luke called, "Ready," Lacy quickly wrapped her arms around the lad's middle, and as the sled gained momentum Lacy's cinnamon sticks flew straight out behind her and slapped in the air like whips. The ride soon ended, and the boy and girl climbed the hill, breathless and enthusiastic. As the young couple neared the top, Annabelle reached out and pulled the little girl to flat ground.

"What a ride! And Hank's the best. He blocked more wind than Lonnie." Hank, upon hearing the words, wore a grin wide as the prairie.

The day passed by too quickly. Back at the home, happy children turned into grouchy bears that needed to be coaxed into dry clothes. Catherine warmed hot chili, and they gathered for a short period around the hearth, reflecting on the day's events before heading off for bed.

Annabelle and Claire remained long after the others were asleep and gazed into the embers of the fire.

"Are you sorry we came?" Claire asked.

"No, just tired. I was thinking. We're lucky that Mattie took us in, that we didn't have to live in an orphanage. No matter how hard we try, there's just not enough time in the day to give each one the attention they need."

"I don't think it was luck, Annabelle. I believe it was the Lord's plan to take care of us."

"If it was Him, then why did He allow our folks to be killed in the first place?"

"I can't answer that." Claire grew weary of Annabelle's resistant attitude toward God and her own inadequate explanations. "I just know that bad things happen. Sometimes they are the result of sin, but God doesn't make them happen. They just do, unless He intervenes—like He did that time you had your accident. He allowed you to live, Annabelle. He has the power and means to get us through hard times and to make good come from them.

"Anyway, because of what we have experienced, we can be of help to these children who are going through similar times. See, there will always be accidents, always sickness, always things that take away parents and leave children orphaned."

"I know what you're trying to say, Claire. I just don't know if I believe it."

"Perhaps you should think heavily on it, Annabelle. You've got saddlebags of disappointments you're toting around. You'd find life a lot easier if you could hand them over to the Lord."

"Maybe. C'mon, time to turn in, little sister. By the way, you don't write Reverend Hamer's sermons for him, do you?"

Claire rolled her eyes and the girls giggled as they went down the long hallway to their room.

twenty-one

One day near the end of February, Luke came back from Dayton spilling over with news that deeply troubled him. He paced the kitchen floor as he voiced his concerns to Jesse Murdock. Annabelle and Claire listened as they assisted Catherine with food preparations.

"It's awful." Luke threw his arms about in protestation. "They auctioned off two boys this morning at the public sale."

"Lord, have mercy," Catherine exclaimed.

Claire dropped the potato which she was paring, and it rolled into the basin with the peelings. "There must be something that can be done!" she cried.

"I talked to Harper." Luke's face twisted in disgust as he remembered his conversation with the overstuffed man who ran the sale.

"What did he say?" Jesse asked.

"He said selling orphans makes money, feeding orphans takes money." Luke clenched his jaw and tightened his fist. "I told him he'd be sorry if it happened again."

Jesse squinted his fine-featured face, wondering how Harper had taken the threat. "He laughed," Luke said.

Catherine turned to her young husband with concern. "What can we do, Jesse?"

"I guess I'll go see Reverend Hamer."

"I already tried that. He's out of town until late tonight."

"Well," Jesse said with determination, "Luke and I will visit the parson first thing in the morning. If he can't do something, then we'll pay the governor a call."

Catherine beamed in admiration at her husband, confident that the two men would accomplish much. Before Annabelle could

115

even take it all in, Neda ran into the room, dripping snow and slush on the kitchen floor. "Come quick, Lacy's sick." The little girl's fright quickened Catherine and Annabelle into action. Together, they followed the young child, stopping only long enough to grab their cloaks from a peg before they braced the winter's cold. The poor girl lay in a heap outside the outhouse door.

Catherine scooped the child up, crooning reassuring words into her ear as she carried her into the house and to the huge room that Lacy shared with the other girls. Placing her on a bunk and stripping off her coat, Catherine ordered, "Get a basin of hot water and a rag." Annabelle flew to do the woman's bidding and sent Luke back into town after the doctor.

Annabelle stayed by Lacy's side and wiped her hot brow with a wet cloth while the young girl whimpered in pain.

Finally, the doctor arrived. "It's her appendix," he quickly diagnosed, and Lacy was taken away in a carriage. Catherine and Jesse accompanied her to the hospital.

It was 11:00 a.m. Claire and Luke waited for news and watched Annabelle pace the floor and wonder if she would see her young friend alive again. Annabelle remembered Lacy's last words as they had carried her away. "Jesus loves me. Mr. Luke says Jesus loves me." Now Annabelle turned to look Luke full in the face. He saw her troubled expression.

"Annabelle?"

"Lacy said you told her Jesus loves her."

"He does. Whatever happens to Lacy, you can be assured that Jesus loves her."

"What if . . . if she dies?"

"Then she'll be in His arms. She'll be very happy. Nothing on earth could be as satisfying."

"I know. Living just brings pain."

"Not always, but even the happy times aren't totally fulfilling. Only spiritual things can truly satisfy."

Annabelle hung her head. "Luke, sometimes I just don't think

I can go on living."

Luke knelt in front of the struggling woman and took her hands in his. Annabelle felt helpless to the point of nausea. He gave her hands a squeeze and the Holy Spirit used his tenderness to move her.

Overcome with tears, she fell into his arms. Claire looked at Luke with pleading, misty eyes as he held Annabelle, who wept upon his shoulder. Succumbing to disappointment and loneliness, Annabelle sobbed uncontrollably.

Finally, Luke spoke. "Annabelle, it is time for you to ask Jesus to come into your life. Allow Him to bring you comfort." She nodded, and he began to pray. She repeated his words in choking little gasps. "Forgive me for my sins. Jesus, come into my life."

As Annabelle spoke the halting words, she felt a peace infiltrating her lightheaded body, and she marveled at it. The burden immediately lifted, and she could not remember why she had not wanted to live. A little spring of joy bubbled in her chest, filling her with hope. "Is this His love?" she asked.

Claire embraced her sister joyfully. "Yes!" she reassured her.

"Now I understand. But I can't explain it."

"It's called faith," Luke said grinning. "It just wells up within us, and we know that God is real."

"Yes!"

The three of them were still awake when Catherine and Jesse returned from the hospital with the sad news that little Lacy had died on the operating table. Her appendix had burst. Annabelle said bravely, "I have experienced new life, and my little sweetheart is experiencing new life, too, with Jesus. Oh, I wish I could go with her." Her heart burned, and tears streamed down her face anew.

"Jesus needs us here," Luke said.

Annabelle nodded. "I will be faithful. Jesus is all I have now."

Claire knew that in time, Annabelle would discover many things worth living for. But it hurt her, also, to let Lacy go. She went to Annabelle. "Come, let's get some sleep." Claire led her away.

Over the next few weeks, Annabelle grieved for her little friend. She talked to Jesus about Lacy. It helped. "Don't let anyone call her hair red, Lord. She likes to call it cinnamon." Annabelle devoured the Bible, spending many hours discussing it with Claire at night in their room. Her newfound faith strengthened the ties between them.

One night Claire suggested to her sister, "I think you should write to Mattie and Kate and tell them what has happened to you."

Annabelle quickly agreed. Then she added, "I believe I shall write a letter to Thaddeas as well." As she fell asleep, she transcribed the letter in her mind.

Dear Thaddeas,

A wonderful thing happened to me, and I want to share it with you. I asked Jesus to come into my life, and He did. It is truly amazing, and now I understand so many things that I did not before. I realize how foolish and selfish I was and want to ask you for your forgiveness. Also, I offer congratulations on your upcoming marriage and hope you will be happy.

I am living in Dayton now. Claire and I came in February to help at the orphanage. I have learned that the real "treasures" in life are not those which money can buy. My most precious jewel was a little girl named Lacy that I met here at the orphanage. She lives in heaven now with Jesus. Her short life brought so much beauty to mine. She was the instrument the Lord used to show Himself to me.

I just wanted you to know these things since you were praying for me. I knew it would make you happy. Whether we meet again on this earth, or in heaven, I remain, forever yours,

Annabelle

twenty-two

Annabelle visited Lacy's grave site. She watched the March wind blow hard across the tiny plot, creating snow drifts, and remembered the day they had gone sledding and smiled. As she knelt to brush the snow away from the evergreen wreath, resting against the small grave marker, she fingered the words carved into the wooden memorial: "Lacy Gray, a precious little jewel, born April, 1799, died February 27, 1808."

Remembering Lacy and her courage in mothering her tiny sisters, Neda and Missy, she wondered where the girls' parents were and if they would ever find out that their child was dead. Annabelle thought about her own parents, who had died at such a young age. She imagined Lacy looking for them in heaven to tell them all about Claire and herself. Lacy knew about them for they had talked about many things.

Fast-sailing clouds cast a shadow across the grave's marker, and Annabelle looked toward the heavens. The sun peeked out for a split second, and the moisture on the bare limbs that hung overhead glittered. Just as quickly, the brilliance disappeared, displaying branches dull gray and white with snow. "That's what you were, Lacy, a glimpse of heaven's beauty."

Now that Annabelle was a Christian, there was so much to learn. She marveled anew at her peace of mind and thanked God for His love. It was as if everything had purpose now, even the pain. Annabelle put her heart, soul, and body into the work at the orphanage and soaked up the words from the Bible like a sponge. Sometimes she asked Claire or Luke questions about what she read. She came to greatly admire Luke—his intelligence about spiritual things, his enthusiasm around the orphanage.

She started back to the home, and her tracks filled with the drifting snow. Upon returning, she hung up her coat and went to the kitchen to lend a hand. At the open doorway, she overheard Jesse and Luke talking in the adjoining parlor. When she heard what they were saying, she stopped to listen for the subject greatly interested her.

"Reverend Hamer gave me several options. We can make a deal with Harper, assuring him we will buy all children up for sale and requiring him to report them to us immediately. Or, we could get up a petition with as many signatures as possible and deliver it personally to the governor in Chillicothe. The problem really isn't just local, you know. Of course, moving toward this larger scale plan means finding willing people to house these children. Perhaps it would be a step toward state funding of orphanages."

"Or even federal funding. You're right, Luke. It's not a local problem. That makes the first option a feeble one. Harper can't be trusted anyway. He would probably up his price and still try to make money off the innocents. But I imagine we'll be forced to start with that option while working toward the other."

"That is exactly what I was thinking, Jesse. It takes time to get things moving in Congress." The two men shook hands in an unspoken pact of the heart.

Annabelle realized she had totally forgotten about the problem. Lacy's sickness and death had all but erased the issue from her mind. She thought if anyone could change things for the better it would be Jesse and Luke. She turned to go until she heard Jesse ask, "Any other news?"

"I heard that the Indians camped up at Greenville, under Tecumseh and the Prophet, are having it real hard this winter. Women and children are starving. Hundreds of Indians arrived without thought of hunting grounds or survival."

"Why are they gathering? It doesn't make sense."

"The Army thinks they plan to attack. They expect an uprising. The government is soon going to make them dispel, run them out of there."

"They could be innocent, Luke. Maybe they are banding together for religious ceremonies. I hope the Army doesn't break up their camp right in the middle of winter."

"Reverend Hamer said the Lebanon Shakers are getting some food together to take to the camp. He is going to speak to his parishioners to try and get some additional donations. Most folks don't like helping Indians though, so I don't know how much success he'll have."

"Wish there was something we could do. But we're operating on donations ourselves."

Luke nodded in understanding. "I could write my father a letter. Maybe his church could help some. But, again, folks are stubborn as stumps when it comes to Indians . . . except the Galloways." Luke thought a minute. "I'll mention Galloway to Father in my letter. Perhaps he could head a group to round up some food."

Annabelle shuddered. Greenville was not that far away. She was not sure that helping Indians was the right thing to do, but she knew her friend, Rebecca Galloway, was close friends with the Indian chief they were talking about, Tecumseh. Annabelle had seen the Indian in Beaver Creek a few times. He was quite handsome. Rebecca had often sung his praises to Annabelle.

Thinking about her friend reminded her of Dorie Cooper. She had not thought of her in months. Annabelle considered writing her old friend a letter to share what had been happening in her life. *Dorie will never believe it!* she mused. Catherine interrupted Annabelle's daydream, summoning her to the kitchen.

৯

The wind howled like a wild beast, and limbs clawed outside the window of the room Annabelle shared with Claire. Annabelle thought she had never waited so long for spring to appear when the children could play outdoors without the hassle of coats, mittens, and boots. The days seemed so short, with never enough hours to get things done. After the children's classroom lessons, it was supper time, then bedtime. Annabelle pined for the longer, carefree days of summer, but did not consider going home to Beaver Creek.

twenty-three

April sun rays thawed the Dayton area. Trees shook off their wrappings of snow and ice, making streams of the winter's precipitations. Rivulets forged downhill, joining neighboring tributaries. This merging of forces enlarged their beds and bolstered their flow until they were indeed a great force that dumped into the mightier branches of the Miami, Stillwater, and Mad rivers—even Wolf Creek was of worthy magnitude.

Word spread quickly throughout the city of dangerous water levels. And then the dreaded thing came, April showers. The watercourses continued to swell and gobble up embankments and shorelines.

The children grew restless, unable to play outdoors. Annabelle bounced Cody on her lap while she sought to divert them with a story. A sudden burst of thunder cracked, sounding so close that the children's faces paled and their eyes widened. Before she could reassure them, the door to the main entrance burst open and Luke and Jesse bolted in. The rain behind them dumped in pailfuls and the water rushed off their coats and boots, making puddles all around them.

Jesse stooped to unbuckle his heavy, mud-laden boots. Annabelle realized the men's hair and clothes were soaked and sternly admonished them, "Better get out of those clothes quick, before you catch cold."

"No time. Where is Catherine?" Jesse asked.

Annabelle pointed toward the kitchen and watched the anxious man leave the room. Then she turned to Luke. "What is it?"

"It's bad, real bad. The water is flooding the main streets, people are running for their lives. Buildings are collapsing, belongings going downriver."

Annabelle gasped, "No!"

"Will the water come here?" Barney asked.

"Not yet. We need to pray that it will quit raining. In the meantime, Jesse and I are going back to the church. It's on high ground for the time being and folks are taking refuge there. You women will have to double up the children and make room. I'm sure we'll be bringing some folks to spend the night."

Catherine Murdock followed her husband to the door and forced the men to drink large drafts of coffee before they braved the storm again. Catherine kissed Jesse and they spoke in low tones. Annabelle turned to Luke.

"Luke."

He looked down at her and smiled. "Yes."

"Be careful . . . and . . . and God be with you."

"Thank you, Annabelle. I'll be fine." Moments later they were gone, two lone men taking arms against the elements. Annabelle looked at Catherine with a fearful expression. Catherine straightened.

"Come, there is much to be done," she said.

≈

That night several families sought shelter at the orphanage. Some Catherine put up in beds, but the rest just found spots on the floor. She, Claire, and Annabelle kept busy serving coffee and drying out clothes by the fire. Annabelle was grateful that Mattie had initiated the comforter project at Reverend Wheeler's church. When the new comforters they brought for the children had arrived, the old ones were stored away. Now these were rummaged out, and the room stank of wet bodies, wool, and firewood.

With all of the excitement, the children were hard to bed down. They made new friends among the stranded and were wound tight as clocks. Long past midnight, Claire and Annabelle tucked the last child in and prayed for the twelfth time—once per child—that the Lord would make the rain cease.

"If the Lord hears the prayers of children, then surely this request will be answered," Claire said as she rubbed a kink out of her neck.

"He listens to the prayers of children. Remember your prayer, when I had my wagon accident," Annabelle reminded her.

"Yes. Now what we need is faith that He will do a miracle."

"I believe," Annabelle said. "I have this feeling. When we prayed for Lacy, it was not the same. I think I knew what His answer was going to be. But something within is welling up, this . . . this faith."

"Good." Claire gave her sister a hug. How thankful she was that Annabelle was now a sister in Christ, as well.

When they reached the end of the hallway, and just before they reached the parlor, they heard a knock on the door. Annabelle quickly pulled it open, anticipating more stranded townsfolk. What she saw was a drenched blond man, holding a crying child tightly against his chest.

"Luke!"

She pulled him in out of the storm, and he placed the soaked bundle into her arms. "Can you get her dry and rock her?"

Annabelle nodded and carried the small child to her own room, where she clothed the little girl in warm clothes. Singing softly, she rocked her from the edge of her bed, then whispered, "Jesus loves you, little jewel."

When Claire went to bed she found Annabelle and the youngster curled up together. She covered them with Annabelle's quilt, pulling her own heavy limbs into her bunk for at least an hour's sleep before the morning's dawn.

☙

Annabelle opened heavy eyes and would have cried for joy if she had not remembered the sleeping child lying at her side, for the sun shone, sending beams of comfort into her room.

She eased out of bed and fell to her knees. "Thank you, Lord. Thank you."

❧

Annabelle supervised the children's play and reflected on the happenings of the past week. The first few days had been crazy. There were so many mouths to feed, many extra helping hands, more children underfoot. She was grateful they soon were able to let them run out of doors.

Each day the men staying at the orphanage accompanied Jesse and Luke into the city to rescue, restore, and rebuild. First, suitable shelter was found for the homeless. The cleanup seemed endless, and the new construction costly. Every day folks prayed that the sun would keep shining and it did.

The ground was still mushy-soft, which was the reason Annabelle did not hear Luke approach. She jumped when she felt his hand touch her shoulder.

"Sorry, I didn't mean to frighten you."

Annabelle relaxed. "I didn't hear you come." She looked back at the children playing. "They are so happy to be outside again. Look how free they are."

"Thank you."

"For what?"

"For all your help, your work. You pitched in and did the work of two during this disaster."

"I couldn't do enough."

"I know. I felt that way too. Especially when Clara's parents were killed. If only I had gotten there sooner." He spoke of the little girl he had brought to Annabelle the night of the flood.

"But you saved her life!" Luke warmed under the encouragement of Annabelle, always so vibrant and spunky. He remembered how it used to get her into trouble and was pleased that she had learned to channel all that energy into helping others.

Wanting to express his affirmation, Luke reached out and placed his hands upon her shoulders. "Annabelle, the Lord's done a mighty work in you. You have become quite a woman."

The praise embarrassed Annabelle and she dropped her eyes momentarily and blushed. His kiss, then, came unexpectedly, and it was so gentle that she wondered if she had imagined it.

Since her conversion, she had come to have great respect and admiration for Luke. She felt a glowing happiness that he paid her such a compliment. He smiled at her now, and his gaze almost unnerved her. Then he spoke softly.

"I got a letter today from Ben. You can read it if you like. It says that he and Kate are ready to adopt Cody and Gabe."

Annabelle's green eyes sparkled with joy. "Oh! I'm so glad."

"Me, too." Luke looked over his shoulder and heaved a great breath. "I better get back to work. There's still so much to do. I'll see you tonight at supper, Annabelle."

The way he said her name made her wonder. Was it her imagination, or was there something special about it?

twenty-four

"I cannot believe it is coming to this. Everything Father worked for is crumbling." Thaddeas paced the dining room floor, addressing Leon and Amelia.

"It's not that bad, Son. Things are not falling apart, yet. It just seems so because the responsibility lies partially on your shoulders."

Leon listened to his brother rant for several minutes. In the short time he had worked with Thad, he had learned it was best to let him vent all his feelings before offering any advice. Now he intervened.

"I think the best thing we can do is close down the shop for awhile, Thad. It does not make sense to be pulling money out of our investments to make goods that will just sit in a warehouse."

Tears glistened in Amelia's eyes. Having been through worse times with her husband, she knew they would survive this, but it touched her to watch her grown-up sons make such decisions. She was proud of them.

Thaddeas nodded. "You're right, of course. Maybe we should pull all the goods out of the School Street warehouse, then, and keep them at the storefront since we can't get out of the rent for another six months anyway."

"Good idea. And, Thad, we'll go together when we tell our employees. It's hard, but there just isn't any other way."

"Do you want to go now?"

"Why don't we let them finish the day?"

With business temporarily resolved, Amelia spoke.

"Thaddeas, a letter came for you from Dayton."

"Dayton? The only person I know there is Luke Wheeler. I wonder why he is writing." Amelia handed her son the letter and he walked away with it, mounting the stairs that led to his room.

Seating himself at his desk, he took a look at the letter in his hand. There was no return address. *That is strange,* he thought. He opened the letter and quickly turned to the last page to see who it was from. *Annabelle!*

His excitement mounted, despite himself. With trembling hands he shuffled the pages back to the beginning. Thaddeas cried when he read about Annabelle's conversion, her apology, and her new outlook on life. She mentioned his prayers. Sobs overtook him and he pushed the letter aside, burying his face in his hands.

Oh, that he could be there to see the change in her. He marveled over the miracle of her conversion and tried to envision what she might be like. In his wildest dreams, he could not imagine her working at an orphanage.

With the need to be alone and think this thing through, he gathered his wraps and started toward the docks. First, he passed through the residential area, a row of brownstone houses occupied by wealthy merchants like his own family. The afternoon sun shone on the manicured wet lawns, creating fields of diamonds.

He wondered how many of these folks dealt with the same problem in their businesses that his family encountered with their leather shop. But his mind did not stay on business long. It returned to the letter from Annabelle. *Helping orphans! I can't believe it!*

Reaching Dorchester Road, he picked up his gait and in no time approached the docks. The familiar sight stretched before him. The fog, which had lifted around noon, allowed the city's shame to manifest itself, the result of the despised Embargo Act.

The docks were jammed, crowded with freighters and cargo ships as well as a hodgepodge of smaller vessels. Sailors slopped the decks for want of something better to do. A group of burly, unkempt men drank and yelled obscenities. When Thaddeas walked past them, one called out, "Cost ya to walk on this here deck. Be off with ya, ya no good 'monger, unless ya got some goods ta ship." This set the others into a gale of laughter. Thaddeas looked away until he passed them. The whole scene disgusted him. *It's best when this place is fogged over,* he thought.

Seagulls swooped down and shrieked out, adding their soprano to the bass of the waves hitting against the crafts and docks. Thaddeas stopped to watch the birds pick through the dirt and sand, then soar across the water, diving to come up with a fish. The smell of salt, fish, fowl, and sea was potent, but it did not call out to him. It was the land across the mountains that whispered his name.

Thaddeas realized how weary he had become of Boston, the sea, the politics. In that moment, he vowed to take Mary Beth west. A rush of excitement hit him. They would move up the wedding date! He knew that Leon was capable of handling things here.

Thaddeas made an about-face and ran until he hailed a carriage and, breathless, tried to calm himself as he gave the driver Mary Beth's address on Walnut Street. Within twenty minutes he was standing at her front door.

"Come in, Mr. Larson," the maid invited.

"Could you tell Mary Beth that I am here?"

"Certainly."

He rubbed his arms and shifted feet as he waited.

"Thaddeas!"

"Hello, can we talk?"

"Of course, come into the parlor. You're as nervous as a rabbit. What's wrong, Thaddeas?"

"Nothing is wrong. I just came to an important decision . . . about our future, Mary Beth."

"Sit down, please. What is it?"

"We are going to speed up our wedding date and move to the West . . . as soon as possible."

"I don't understand. Why this sudden decision?" Mary Beth had deliberately set their marriage date far into the future, hoping Thaddeas' love would take on more fullness. He was passionate enough, vibrant energy coursed through his sturdy, well-built body, but Mary Beth knew she did not possess his love, and did not know why. Could a man like this only love adventure? Or was there a woman from his past who already owned his heart? He was so commanding, so impulsive. It frightened her.

Hoping his restlessness would settle over the months of their engagement, she had waited expectantly to see the shine of love in his eyes. There was a gleam there today, but from what she did not know.

"Things aren't going well at the leather shop. You know that. There is really no reason for me to stay here any more. I am itching to go west."

"How soon?"

"As soon as you can arrange things."

Mary Beth acted out of character, for she picked up a nearby cushion and hurled it at him. It caught him square in the head, ruffling his black wavy hair. He gaped at her in amazement. "Mary Beth!"

"You exasperate me!" she screamed.

"Mary Beth, I'm sorry. You said that you would follow me wherever I wanted to go. I . . . I thought you would be happy."

She quickly gained her composure as a new revelation hit her. "Thaddeas! I know what it is. I finally know what it is. You are running away from something. That's it, isn't it?"

"Nonsense."

"I shall not even marry you at all unless you tell me everything."

When Thaddeas realized she was serious, he spoke. "I feel like I'm on a raft fighting against the current—going in the wrong direction—but I can't remember why it's the wrong way."

"Perhaps you are running from love." Mary Beth referred to their own relationship, meaning to encourage him to open up to the love between them.

"No, that's over."

"What?"

"That was over months ago. How did you know?"

She took a deep breath, and courageously forged ahead. They were so close. If they could just talk this out. "Please tell me about her."

"My cousin, from Beaver Creek. I thought I loved her, but she had different ideas. She was a gold-seeker, with lofty ambitions."

"And you wanted her to love you and not your money."

"Yes. She sent me a telegram, pursuing me, and I dismissed her. Since then, you came into my life and, now, you are all to me."

"I wish I could believe that. Did she free you then?"

"Yes. In fact, I continued to pray for her, that she would become a Christian, and now she has. So I am totally free from her and any obligations toward her."

The light dawned in Mary Beth's brain. "When did you find out that she had become a Christian?"

"Just recently. Mary Beth, why does it matter?"

"I believe the reason you feel you are riding the current in the wrong direction is because you need to find out if she has indeed changed." Mary Beth gathered her courage. "Running off to the wilderness probably won't solve your problems. And I am sure of one thing—I won't be accompanying you. I am not so hard up, so needy, that I have to marry someone who loves another. You are not the only available man in Boston, Thaddeas Larson! And you better leave this house before I throw something harder than a pillow!"

"Darling, be reasonable."

"Don't call me darling. The way I see it you have several choices. You may rot in Boston. You can fly to your wilderness. Or you can look up that old flame. It is nothing to me, for we are no longer engaged. Weigh your decision wisely, Thaddeas. Don't make another mistake!" She left him alone in the parlor.

Thaddeas was mortified. Then a grin spread across his face. *Thank you, Mary Beth,* he said to himself as he left the two-story stone home. He knew what this had cost her. Could he allow her to make this sacrifice? He had no other choice. "You're an angel," he called, feeling happier than he had in months.

twenty-five

"If a farmer had a milk cow, two sheep, ten chickens, and one hound dog, how many animals would he have altogether?" Luke posed the question to the group of young boys seated before him.

Barney dangled his legs, made some scratches on his slate, then raised his hand.

"Yes, Barney?"

"Would that there cow be a Guernsey or a Holstein?"

Annabelle smiled as she watched Luke patiently answer the towheaded boy.

"The cow is Guernsey, there is a white sheep and a black lamb, nine Rhode Island Red hens, one Rhode Island rooster, and one short-tailed hound dog used for hunting coon, and oh yes, three baby chicks just hatched."

"Aw, look what ya did, Barney. You made the problem harder," complained nine-year-old Logan.

Slates squeaked as the children added up the sums, and Luke gave Annabelle a knowing smile. She moved methodically behind the boys to see if they placed their number columns straight, and stopped to help Barney line up his one hound dog under the one Rhode Island Red rooster.

The dinner bell rang, and the children scrambled to line up at the door. "Think about this over lunch," Luke told his pupils. "See you back here at one o'clock sharp. You may go now."

Annabelle watched Luke with wonder, marveling at the way he commanded the children's respect, yet kept the lines of communication open. Any of the orphans could flee to him with a concern, except for the older girls who were beginning to show signs of shy adolescence.

She thought about them now, and wondered what would become of them. How would they find husbands, stuck away in a place like this? Amity slipped past Luke just then, taking a quick peek at his face. He smiled at the fourteen-year-old girl, and she dropped her eyes to the floor as she hurried past him. Annabelle realized the girl was enamored, probably had a crush on the teacher.

Annabelle considered this. *I wonder if he knows.* He is good looking and young. Maybe he grew the mustache to look older. She had always deemed him better-looking than his brother, Ben. Her eyes took in his tall, lean frame, blond hair, and face that was both tanned and freckled. *Those blue eyes would melt any young girl's heart, even though they are never flirty.* The sapphire pools gave his face a kind, attentive expression.

"Thinking hard on something?" Luke asked as he waited for her to join him.

"About you." She reddened. "You're a good teacher, Luke. In fact, you're a good preacher too."

"Well, that is high praise. And what might you be after?"

Annabelle socked him in the arm, then blushed again as she felt his solid muscles flex beneath her fist. He reached out playfully and snagged her closed hand in the palm of his enormous one, holding it for a moment then releasing it like a hot branding iron.

She thought he acted differently toward her lately and could not figure it out. She shrugged it off. "When will Ben and Kate come for the boys?" she questioned.

"I thought maybe we would deliver them."

"Really?" she squealed in delight.

"Would that please you?" He watched her reaction.

"Oh yes! It would be so good to go home."

His eyebrows arced. This creature was not the same girl that he had once considered shallow and immature. He enjoyed her company now, as well as her helping hands, and hoped she was not homesick.

"I mean for a visit. And Claire will be glad, too. Or, maybe I should ask, who will be going?"

"No plans are set, I've just been rolling ideas around. It's still too muddy to take a wagon; however, it shouldn't be long until we can make the trip. I imagine the Murdocks can do without the three of us for a short while. The volunteers at church like to fill in occasionally. This will give them the opportunity."

"When will you tell the children, Cody and Gabe?"

"Soon."

"Just think, they'll be our nephews."

"I can't wait to see them smothered with Kate and Ben's love."

"Me too."

Luke's expression changed, "Oh, I wanted to tell you something."

"Yes?"

"Jesse and I talked to Harper. He agreed to cooperate. He gave us his word he won't sell any more stranded children, but we have to pay him to take them in at the orphanage." Luke looked concerned. "I don't trust the man."

"But that is wonderful, Luke. I'm so proud of you and Jesse."

"I guess it's the best we can do. We're starting a petition to work toward changes on a larger scale. Do you want to sign it?"

"Of course."

Luke gave her an intense look. Annabelle met his gaze, sensing that Luke was evaluating her and appraising her with high marks, and it felt good.

ও

Claire hung her dress on the hook beside her bunk and slipped her flannel nightgown over her blond head. She did not climb under the covers, but perched on the edge of her mattress with her elbows on her knees, watching her sister brush her hair. She watched the copper tresses elongate and then spring back when Annabelle pulled the brush away.

"You happy here, Annabelle?"

"Yes. Are you?"

"Mm hm. You've changed so much. I never know what to expect from you."

"I have? I was pretty awful, wasn't I?"

"No, of course not."

"I could never understand how you could be so caring for folks. Take for instance, Sammy Hawkes."

"What about him?"

"See what I mean. You always defended him, always went out of your way to encourage him, just because he stuttered."

"The other children teased him."

Annabelle nodded. "But I didn't care. I only considered my own needs. Since Jesus changed my heart, I regret my past."

"It's all forgiven. Kate will like the changes in you."

"I'd love to have a nice long chat with her."

"Soon enough, you'll be able to when we take that vacation and visit home."

"I can hardly wait."

"Annabelle?"

"Mm hm." Annabelle laid her brush aside and wiggled under the covers of her bed.

"I think Luke is falling in love with you."

"What?"

"You heard me."

Annabelle sat up straight. "Oh, I hope not! That will ruin everything."

"I don't think it would be such a bad thing to have a man like Luke love you." Claire's voice took on a dreamy quality.

"I am not ready to love anyone, Claire," Annabelle said sternly. "Loving a man hurts like having your insides full of burrs. I'm not ready to go through that pain again."

"Oh, Annabelle," Claire giggled. "I hope it is not like that. Just forget I said anything and go to sleep."

But Annabelle could not sleep.

twenty-six

"I want to thank all of you who helped out with the food for the Indians at Greenville." Reverend Wheeler gazed long and hard at his Beaver Creek congregation. Some squirmed in their seats, but remained quiet. No one had nerve enough to disagree with the mission project in this setting. But the reverend knew that as soon as the service was over, many would complain and criticize the project; that is why his gaze bore down relentlessly on several of his parishioners.

James Galloway patted his daughter's hand and exchanged a meaningful glance with his wife. He remained one of the few who had pitched in to help the preacher head up this particular charitable outreach.

Rebecca's thoughts turned to the proud Indian, Tecumseh. He was her good friend. It hurt her to see him have to take donations from the white men to feed his people. His braves were proud, and able to provide for their own. However, the government had cruelly hemmed them in, continually taking away more rights. Her eyes watered as she listened to the preacher conclude his message and say the benediction over the congregation.

"The Lord bless you. Go in peace."

Outside the school house, the day burst with the new growth of springtime. Folks gathered in familiar circles to visit. Kate overheard one mother remark, "A body can surely tell that the children have spring fever. Jest look at 'em. I wonder how the teacher can give them any learnin' this time of year."

Nearby, Melanie Whitfield rubbed her swollen stomach—to make a statement, Kate thought. "This baby sure does move a lot. I think being pregnant is just the closest thing to heaven a body can be."

Kate nodded. "When's the little one due?"

"I expect around August."

"You're mighty big for August."

Melanie's face flushed and her eyes glared, hot as two volcanoes. "Might be twins."

Kate nearly giggled. She should not have said that, but sometimes that woman got under her skin. "Wouldn't that be nice," she said sweetly.

Ben had come up behind her and overhearing Melanie's last statement, interrupted the conversation. "We just might be having twins ourselves."

"What!" Melanie clapped her hand across her mouth in astonishment. "Well, glory be!"

"Ben, you better explain yourself," Kate admonished her husband, but on the inside she was enjoying their little joke.

"We're adopting two boys, Melanie, from Luke's orphanage."

"Oh. Well I wondered, didn't think you'd be having real children, so long as it's been and everything."

Kate became indignant. "These are real children, Melanie. Two very sweet little boys."

"Why, of course they are, honey. I didn't mean no harm by it. I just ain't myself when I'm with child, I guess."

Kate thought she seemed very much like herself.

Ben gave his wife a supportive caress and moved away to join a group of men. As he drew closer, he saw forceful arm movements and heard explosions of anger as the men grumbled their opinions. "We're feeding the very hands that are going to shoot arrows in our backs, burn our homes, and scalp our families." Ben turned and walked away. This kind of talk discouraged him.

❧

On the ride home, Ben and Kate discussed the sermon and
Melanie Whitfield. Eventually the conversation led to Cody
and Gabe. Kate's eyes sparkled. "I can hardly wait."

"How old is Cody now?"

"Two years old this month, May fourteenth," she said without the slightest hesitation. "I hope they're here for his birthday."

"They will be, Darling." Ben hugged his wife. "Not to change
the subject, but have you noticed how all of Luke's letters sing
the praises of your sister, Annabelle?"

"It's hard to believe, isn't it?" Ben looked at her questioningly and she clarified. "That she has changed that much. We
so quickly forget God's power, that His love changes lives. I'm
real anxious to see her again. She may actually seem like
Claire's sister now."

"And yours. Don't sell yourself short, Dear. But what I meant
is . . ." Ben scratched his head and it was Kate's turn to look
puzzled. "Sounds like Luke might be falling in love with her."

Kate smiled. "That would be nice, but I always pictured him
and Claire together."

"I can't believe you've had such thoughts and kept them to
yourself!"

"Only thoughts, Darling. The only romance I'm sure about
is ours."

Ben answered his wife with an affectionate pat on the knee.

❧

The same day, May ninth, Thaddeas arrived in Beaver Creek,
dusty and weary. His legs felt numb and weak as he hobbled to
the front door of Tucker House. It looked so good. He raised
his fist and pounded. Since it was Sunday, Buck and Mattie
were both at home, napping in the sitting room.

"I'll get it." Buck staggered across the room, jumping up
from his sleep a bit too fast. "Just a minute, I'm coming," he
yelled. Then under his breath he muttered, "Don't need to break

down the door."

He pulled it open with a frown, wondering who was disturbing their siesta, and stared full into the unshaven face of his nephew. "Thaddeas! Boy!" He pulled Thad into a bear hug, screaming into the young man's ear, "Mattie, come quick! Thaddeas is home!"

"What!" Mattie scrambled to the door, barely missing Freckles' tail. Her arms flailed with expression, "I can't believe it. Oh, it's so good to see you. Come in."

"We didn't get a letter, so we weren't expecting you," the sheriff stammered.

"Wasn't time to write. I had to get here quick as I could. Started out the first of April and made it in six weeks." Thaddeas seemed proud of himself.

"Why? What was the hurry, Son?"

"I'm home to stay, and I'm going to marry Annabelle."

Buck cleared his throat. "They don't need you in Boston?"

"Nope. We closed down the leather shop because all our goods kept piling up."

"Things got worse?"

Thad nodded. "That Embargo Act is ruining the merchants in the coastal cities." He saw Buck's worried expression and quickly assured him, "Oh, we'll make it all right. We've got plenty to ship as soon as the seas open. In the meantime, Mother and Leon are living off investments. Leon is quite capable of handling affairs at home."

Buck warmed to the idea of having his nephew back and expressed himself, "I'm glad you decided to come home."

"It is home, Uncle Buck. By the way, Mother and Leon send their regards."

Mattie's own motherly instincts toward Thad surfaced. She gave him another hug. "Now, what can I get you? You must be hungry and thirsty."

"I don't suppose you'd have any pie?"

"I sure do. A custard pie."

"And a glass of cold milk?"

Her face crinkled just like he remembered it. "Comin' right up."

Buck studied Thaddeas. "Annabelle and Claire aren't in Beaver Creek anymore. They are helping Luke out at the orphanage. I don't know as any of us will know Annabelle when we see her again. I hear she's made some major changes."

Thaddeas listened attentively. "I'm counting on it."

"And speaking of changes, I thought you were engaged to a girl in Boston."

"That didn't work out, Buck. It never could, because I've always loved Annabelle."

"I see. Well, I wouldn't get your hopes too high."

Thaddeas just laughed. "Uncle Buck, you just wait and see. I'll be needing to get a few supplies before I go on to Dayton," he said, planning out loud.

"You won't need to go to Dayton."

"What do you mean?"

"Luke is bringing Annabelle and Claire home for a visit. Ben and Kate are adopting two little boys from the orphanage and the girls and Luke are bringing them. They should be here within the week."

Thaddeas brightened and hollered, "This is perfect!"

Buck looked amused, "Annabelle will be surprised, all right."

twenty-seven

Buck's strides mashed down the tall fronds of grass growing on the grounds surrounding Green's Sawmill. The ground sloped downward toward the bank of the Little Miami River where the mill, a hub of activity, provided many men with work and wages.

David Green had welcomed Thaddeas back to his old job with open arms, which is where Buck found him wearing a frustrated expression on his face.

"Hello, Uncle."

"Morning, Thaddeas. How's it going?"

"Tough as horseshoes." He bent forward so Buck could hear when he lowered his voice to a whisper. "Books are all messed up. It'll take me awhile to get them straightened out."

Buck grinned. "That's why you looked so troubled when I came in. Well, you're just the man to do the job."

"Thanks, Buck."

"You bet. I thought you might like to know . . . Annabelle is back."

The quill in Thaddeas' hand snapped in two. "What! She is?"

Sunday's confident man suddenly looked like a whipped puppy. Buck compassionately reassured him. "Don't worry, Son. You'll do fine."

"Does she know I'm here?"

"No. Thought we'd let that be a surprise."

Thad nodded as he nervously toyed with the broken quill pieces. "Maybe that is best. Meet her head on before she has time to rationalize. Get her true reaction that way."

143

"There's a birthday party at Kate and Ben's tonight. Can you come?"

"Whose birthday?"

"Cody. One of the little boys Ben and Kate are adopting."

"Oh! Yes. I'll be there."

"Good." Buck slapped his nephew roughly on the back. "Now, you better get back to work."

"If I can concentrate."

a

Annabelle looked out her bedroom window; Tucker House seemed just the same. A robin flew with string in its bill and lit upon the budding limb of the hickory nut tree, then disappeared within its foliage. "Missed the tulips this year," she muttered to herself.

She examined the few clothes she had brought back from Dayton, trying to decide what to wear to Cody's birthday party. Fingering a soft green gown she had not worn for months, she thought, *I'll wear that, then just leave it here. Not much need for such niceties at the orphanage.* She concluded, *It'll be fun to dress up tonight. I think I'll leave my hair down. It's so bothersome always binding it up.* Catherine encouraged the girls to do so at the orphanage. *Hope Catherine is not overworked without us.* She sighed.

They had arrived late the night before, bunking at Ben's. Luke explained that the boys might be frightened to be left alone with their new parents. Then this morning, Luke had brought Claire and Annabelle to Tucker House, where they were greeted warmly with hugs and kisses all around.

Luke agreed to stay on at Tucker House for the extent of their visit, giving Ben and Kate time alone with their new family members. However, he had ridden off about an hour earlier to see his father, Mary, and the boys, saying he would meet them back at Ben's that evening.

Suddenly, Annabelle felt hungry. Deciding to go to the

kitchen and find an apple before dressing, she found Mattie bent over the ironing board. "Let me do that," Annabelle offered.

Mattie grinned at Annabelle, then shook her head. "Nope. Not today. Consider it a holiday."

"But it isn't."

"Seems like it, having you girls home. I missed you. Best sit down, so we can talk a spell."

Annabelle grabbed an apple out of a shallow wooden bowl that graced the center of the table, eyeing Mattie all the time and wondering what she had to say.

Annabelle crunched a bite out of her apple just as Mattie spoke.

"You happy, Annabelle?"

"Yes." Annabelle choked and coughed, and Mattie ordered, "Git yerself a drink."

Annabelle's apple rolled to the floor. "Now, there's no use wastin' a good apple," Mattie teased.

"Sorry, Mattie." Annabelle picked up the red fruit and washed it off in a basin of water by the kitchen window.

"Sure is lonely here without you girls."

"Consider it a reprieve. It's about time you had a break, Mattie. You've been such a patient mother."

At the word "mother," Mattie's conscience pricked her. "I love you girls," was all she said.

❧

It was quite a reunion at Ben's. Emmett Wheeler's family was there and, of course, the Tucker House group. Kate made everyone feel at home, and Annabelle just knew her sister would make a perfect mother. She noticed, though, that Gabe and Cody acted like lost little boys, excited yet unsure.

"You boys behaving?" Annabelle asked with a serious expression.

"We played today. Ben showed us horsies," Gabe answered

as he jumped onto her lap. Cody followed Gabe wherever he went and wiggled his body against hers. Her skirt tugged in his tiny grip, and she gently lifted him and pried the material out of his fists, settling the child in the tiny space remaining that his brother did not occupy.

Kate's eyes followed the boys constantly, and now Annabelle saw a glimpse of sadness in the brown pools and knew her sister longed to have them prefer her in such a way. "Oh, look what your mommy has." Annabelle pointed toward Kate and gave them a little pat and a shove, setting them in her direction.

Nearby, she overheard Luke discussing the Indian situation with his father. "Thanks for helping out. I know what you were up against. Folks around Lebanon practically lynched some of the Shakers that drove the wagon loads of food to the settlement." A mournful cry of Ben's beagle interrupted the conversation.

The dog howled again, then let out some short barks, so Ben went to the door and welcomed the visitor. Annabelle heard the familiar voice of Thaddeas and almost cried at the sound. *It could not be. Thaddeas? No one mentioned that he was home. Calm.* She must remain calm.

Suddenly, she felt ashamed and embarrassed at the telegram and letter she had written him. How forward she had been. She must not appear that way now. Annabelle silently vowed she would not let him see the love in her eyes; she would not ruin his life again. So desperately, she longed to make a new start, to have his friendship. But could she stand the pain of it, without his love?

When Thaddeas laid eyes on Annabelle, all of his big talk to his Uncle Buck was just that—talk. He took in the wavy copper tresses. How he had dreamed about their silkiness. Her face glowed, as if a halo floated overhead. He grew tongue-tied and ill at ease. Thoughts raced through his mind, *I don't have*

forever, she plans to go back to Dayton. Don't scare her away
again. Maybe she does not feel the same anymore. Oh, why is
it so hot in here?

It seemed like the room faded away as Annabelle watched
him move around, greeting folks. Then he looked directly at
her and came in her direction. Out of the corner of her eye, she
noticed Mattie and Buck whispering.

Oh, he looked wonderful. Had his shoulders always been
that broad? His hair so dark? His eyes so intense? She rose
from her chair and held out her hand to him. He clasped it
tightly. The room grew quiet. "Hello, Annabelle."

"Thaddeas."

At that moment, Luke slipped out the door to get a breath of
fresh air, and Claire followed him. "Wait up." Luke paused
and waited for the young woman to catch up to him. She spoke
bluntly. "I'm sorry, Luke."

"What?"

She tossed her head toward the house. "About Annabelle."

"You don't miss much do you, blue eyes?"

"It's been pretty obvious—to everyone except Annabelle."

"I thought Thad was out of the picture," he admitted. "No
one told me he was in Ohio. He always loved Annabelle. You
think it would be too obvious if I walk a bit?"

"Don't be gone too long." She sadly retreated to the house.
Thad had seated himself at Annabelle's side. Claire marveled
at how her sister's beauty attracted men. At one time she would
have felt a little pity for the man who won Annabelle's heart,
but now any man who loved her sister could be proud. She
knew Annabelle loved Thaddeas. She wondered what he was
doing back. Would he break her heart again? Or, would
Annabelle break Luke's?

They seemed to be in deep conversation. Annabelle was saying, "Are you here for a visit?"

"No, to stay. I'm working at the mill again."

"I'm glad. Is your fiancée here?"

"No! That didn't work out."

"Oh, I'm sorry." She reached out and touched his hand gently. Luke entered the room just in time to observe the tender scene. Thad lowered his voice so the others couldn't hear their conversation. "I would like to explain it to you. I hope I get the chance very soon."

Annabelle still felt jealous of the Boston lady and resisted the urge to reply sarcastically, for she knew better. "I'll only be here a few days, then I'll be going back to Dayton . . . with Luke." Her eyes glanced across the room at Luke. "This was just intended to be a visit; all of my belongings are at the orphanage."

Thaddeas' heart sank. She would return with Luke? Was there a special connotation in the way she glanced Luke's way? Luke stood where he had entered the room, and Thad's eyes locked with his, each regarding the competition.

Thad turned toward Annabelle, "How about a canoe ride before you leave, like old times?"

"That would be perfect," she replied.

"How would tomorrow evening be?" Thaddeas asked.

"I'll look forward to it."

Gabe rushed into Luke's arms. "Daddy," he called, and the blond-haired giant beamed down at him.

"Uncle Luke is right here," he assured the child while providing him with gentle correction. "There's your new daddy," he pointed toward Ben.

Kate called her sons to come to the table so Cody could blow out his birthday candles. "Come, let's light the candles," she coaxed.

Gabe cried. "We want mommy and daddy to sit beside us."

Cody copied his brother and waved his chubby little hands pointing toward the chairs, "Mommy." Everyone in the room understood that he addressed Annabelle.

"Of course we'll sit by you," Luke offered and he reached out to catch Annabelle's hand, pulling her along. He felt Thad's eyes scald his backside, and winked at Annabelle anyway, glad to snatch her away. "Aunt Annabelle," Luke emphasized the "aunt" part, "and Uncle Luke are right here. Now your mother can light those candles."

As the evening proceeded, Luke monopolized Annabelle in a sweet and charming manner, under the guise of making things easier for Cody and Gabe. Thus, Thaddeas was able to observeAnnabelle's new unselfish character as she ministered to the small children. The fact that Annabelle and Luke worked familiarly well together did not go unnoted.

Claire determined to stay out of the love triangle and did not offer any assistance with the youngsters. Instead, she helped to serve the food. However, she kept an eye on Luke's smooth performance.

When the time came for the youngsters to be tucked in for the night, Annabelle went with Kate. She found the opportunity to encourage her sister. "It won't take long for them to warm up to you."

"I know. It's all right, really. I've waited too long to give up easily."

"Me too," Annabelle said softly, thinking of her Boston gentleman.

twenty-eight

Rebecca Galloway knocked on the door of Tucker House, then tapped the side of her riding habit with her fingers in a nervous manner. She sighed with relief when Annabelle answered the door.

"Rebecca! Come in."

"Hello, Annabelle. I heard you were back in town and wondered if you would like to go riding with me?"

"Sure, come up while I change." Annabelle motioned toward her room.

"That's all right, I'll just wait outside. It's such a beautiful day."

"Yes, it is. I'll just be a minute."

❧

Within the hour, Annabelle mounted her horse with an air of expectancy and shouted to Rebecca, "I really missed riding Dusty." She patted the beast's mane, then acknowledged her friend. "What's been happening in your life, Rebecca?"

"You first. Tell me about the orphanage."

"Working there turned out different than I expected."

"In what ways?"

"I guess I learned to think about other folks' needs as well as my own."

"Was it the children?"

Annabelle nodded. "Especially one little girl named Lacy." She smiled and her voice took on a soft quality, "We became very close, and then she died."

"Oh no. I'm sorry."

"But she taught me about Jesus."

"Really?"

"Her and Luke."

"Tell me about Luke." Rebecca rolled her eyes, making romantic insinuations.

"Luke is a remarkable Christian man."

"I haven't seen him for years. Is he still as handsome?"

"Very!" The girls giggled. "But, as I was saying, when I became a Christian my life became meaningful with peace and purpose."

"I am happy for you. Now, where are you taking me?"

"To a very special place." The spot, the same where she had rendezvoused with Charles Harrison so many times, appeared. Today she wanted to see it through forgiving eyes. It was a chapter of her life that needed closure. They dismounted and she sighed with satisfaction as they tied up the horses.

"Over here," she led her friend through a tangle of dense trees and knee-high bushy plants. The path, now grown over with the season's lush explosion of grass and weeds, no longer existed. In a short while, they emerged into a paradise of wild flowers.

"Oh! It's beautiful," Rebecca gasped.

Annabelle was surprised by the daisies that waved smiling faces. The last time she had been here, it had been autumn. "Changes," she murmured.

"What?"

"Oh, nothing. Come on!"

They left the meadow to forge through more forest, then stepped into another open area totally surrounded on three sides by the wooded foliage. The fourth supplied a panorama of the Beaver Creek's blue tongue, flowing swiftly onward. The water level was high. "Let's rest on that log." *That looks the same,* she thought.

"It's gorgeous. How did you find this spot?"

"My secret," Annabelle cautioned. "Now, tell me about yourself."

"All right. But brace yourself." Annabelle gripped the log

with her gloved hands, eyes enlarged with curiosity. "I've had a marriage proposal," Rebecca said, "and I don't know what to do."

"Really? Who?"

"Promise me you won't tell a soul, not anybody?"

"I promise."

"Tecumseh, the Shawnee Indian chief."

Now Annabelle's mouth flew open. "What! I don't know what to say . . . he's very magnificent, I've seen him . . . and powerful."

"And brave, and respected by his people," Rebecca added.

"Do you love him?"

"Yes, madly, but how can I love an Indian?"

"Oh, Rebecca, what will you do?"

"I don't know."

"It is so romantic. How did it happen?"

"In a canoe."

"What?" Annabelle recalled her engagement with Thad that evening to do that very thing. However, Rebecca interrupted her thoughts.

"A canoe. I can't tell you why we were out rowing. It's an Indian secret. But he proposed very gallantly and properly. He said he'd only take one wife, and I'd never have to work like the other squaws because he was the chief and could declare it."

"Well, that's good. But aren't the soldiers expecting a war soon? Do you know what he's doing in Greenville? Is that part of the secret?"

"No. He doesn't divulge information like that. But I'm afraid if I turn him down—which is what I plan to do—it could cause a war."

"Oh, you poor thing. What a predicament! Rebecca, have you told your father?"

"Yes. We've discussed all the options, and he said he'd support me, whatever I decide."

"But of course you can't worry yourself about the outcome. After all, an Indian uprising could just as easily happen if you did marry him. Imagine, fighting against your own family."

"I have." Rebecca said with sadness.

"One never knows what the future holds. If war or peace lies ahead, we can only trust God with it."

"You're right, Annabelle. Talking with you has been helpful." Rebecca patted her friend's hand. "Will you be returning to the orphanage? I know it's selfish of me, but I hope you'll stay. With Dorie gone for so long, and then you, it's been lonely."

"I miss Dorie, too."

"Did you hear about her?"

"No, what?"

"She's engaged to be married to a congressman."

Annabelle shook her curly head. "It doesn't surprise me. But know what? I'm not even jealous."

"You didn't answer my question. Is there a chance you'll stay?"

"I really don't know." She thought about Thaddeas; leaving him again would be painful. The two women were silent for a long time. The sun drizzled warm rays, causing sweat trickles on their brow. Annabelle plucked a wild violet and inhaled deeply. Its sweet perfume intoxicated her with spring's aroma.

Rebecca broke the spell. "Annabelle, something else is troubling me, and I thought you should know."

"What is it?"

"Oh, I hate to say this, but a rumor is spreading around Beaver Creek. It's about Mattie."

"Mattie?"

"Yes. Word has it she's been seen with a man other than the sheriff, a military man. I'm sure there is some explanation. And, if there is, it would be good for Tucker House to put a bug in some ears. Do you know what I mean?"

"I know there's nothing to it. Gone so long, I've no idea

what it could be about. I'll ask her, and we'll get it all straightened out."

"I can imagine the rumors that are going around about me,"
Rebecca sighed.

"Oh, don't fret. You've done nothing wrong."

When they left that place, Rebecca felt encouraged, but
Annabelle continued to poke at the rumor Rebecca mentioned
from every angle, coming up at dead ends.

twenty-nine

Annabelle dismounted and looked toward the house, where she recognized Mattie at a distance, digging in the flower bed. She stabled Dusty and set off toward her. With concern, she slowed her pace when she saw Mattie wrestling with a fistful of ragweed.

When she reached the older woman, she knelt beside her and uprooted some stubborn dandelions. Mattie warned with approval. "You'll git your ridin' clothes soiled."

"Couldn't get any worse. We stopped off by the creek."

"Sure is a nice day."

"Indeed. I think I have spring fever."

"I 'spect you're thinkin' about goin' back to Dayton, the orphanage and all."

"I guess it's always on my mind. I seem to be just living one day at a time."

"That's what we all do, I 'spect."

"There is something that I want to ask you."

"Go ahead, child."

"I really don't know how to say this, but I hear there's a rumor going around town about Tucker House."

Mattie gave her a quizzical glance, and Annabelle continued, ". . . about you and some Army man?"

Annabelle had never seen Mattie look more stricken. She dropped to the grass, limp like the weeds that lay in a heap between them. Calling up courage, Mattie straightened. "I reckon it's time I told ya. I can't live a lie any longer."

Annabelle held her breath, unable to imagine what kind of deception Mattie could mean. She listened carefully as Mattie told her story in a trembling voice that grew stronger as she spoke.

"A long time ago, when I was about your age, I fell in love with Lieutenant Wade Brooks, only he wasn't a lieutenant then. We weren't married, but I got pregnant. My pa, a preacher, kicked me out of the house."

"Oh, Mattie, what did you do? What did the lieutenant do?"

"He skedaddled, and I never heard from him again until a few months ago. Now he wants to know about our child. There ain't nothin' betwixt us now, he's jest been houndin' me."

"What happened to your child, Mattie?"

"This is the hard part ta tell. I gave her to my married sister, Elizabeth, to raise."

"That's not so bad. I can understand that."

"She and her husband were murdered at the Big Bottom Indian massacre." Annabelle stiffened, and Mattie's tears flowed unrestrained, rivers of regret wet her cheeks as she continued. "My child survived. I took her and my sister's own two daughters ta raise as my own."

The truth was hard for Annabelle to accept. "Are you saying . . ."

Mattie nodded. "Kate is my daughter. You and Claire my nieces. That's why I didn't adopt you till after Kate married. She was already mine."

"I-I thought it was because you married Buck that you adopted us. Why?" Annabelle screamed. "Why have you lied to us all these years?"

Mattie hung her head as strangling sobs engulfed her. "I already had my seamstress shop in Beaver Creek. Folks knew me, and I liked it here. I didn't want them ta know about my past."

"How could you? This is unforgivable!" Annabelle rose to leave, but Mattie clung to her skirt, preventing her.

"Wait. There's more." Annabelle glared down at Mattie.

"Lieutenant Brooks, Kate's father, hired Charles Harrison ta spy on us. He was the prowler at Ben's place. That's why he left so abruptly."

"He . . . used me?"

"I'm so sorry." Mattie still clutched Annabelle's riding habit.

Annabelle jerked it loose. "I shall not forgive you!" she cried out and ran for the house.

Annabelle isolated herself in her room, where she wrestled with this new-found information. She stomped, ranted, and raved just like the old creature she used to be then gave in to self-pity and weeping. "Oh, Lord," she moaned, "Kate is not even my sister, she's my cousin. How awful. But Claire . . . yes, she's a sister. Oh, how can this be?"

Eventually, there was a knock on her door. "Go away," she shouted.

"It's Buck."

"What do you want?"

"Thaddeas is here to see you."

"Tell him to go away!" Her mind raced. "Wait! I'll be down in a little while."

"Very well." Buck turned away, relieved that she would see Thaddeas. Things were going badly with Mattie broken and sobbing in one room, and Annabelle angry and weeping in another. If only Claire were here—but Luke had driven her into town.

❧

Annabelle found Thad waiting outside. As she approached, Thad's heart quickened with anticipation for he had planned this evening very carefully, hoping to mend their relationship. Then she drew nearer and he realized something was very wrong.

"Annabelle! What is it?"

"You're never going to believe it."

"Try me," he coaxed.

"Maybe later. I'm not going to let Mattie spoil our canoe ride."

Thad, unwilling to open a new can of worms, quickly agreed, "All right then. Let's go." He offered his hand and she took it as they walked toward the creek.

"Looks like Buck keeps the path worn down fishing," Annabelle observed. The cool air helped her to gain her composure.

"This looks great," Thad breathed deeply, taking in the woodsy freshness. "I missed this place."

The footpath declined then turned sharply, and the couple stepped carefully over the jutting roots from the giant cottonwoods that lined the creek bank. "Uncle Buck said the canoe should be beached along here . . . there it is!" Thad pointed with enthusiasm.

The tip of the craft stuck out from behind a mossy rock. Thad hurried to free the small craft and slid it into the water for Annabelle's inspection. "Madam," he offered. As she entered the canoe, he cautioned, "Carefully now." She positioned herself on the far end and grabbed fast onto the sides. "Ready?" Thad asked.

"All set."

Thad climbed in and pushed off the grassy shore. Within seconds they glided swanlike through the water. Annabelle closed her eyes and relaxed. "This seems like old times, Thad," she murmured.

"We've many memories along this creek, don't we?"

"I do recall outfishing you on numerous occasions," she quipped.

"You would!" Thaddeas exclaimed. Then he ventured, "Annabelle, could we start over, you and I?"

Her heart flopped like the fish beneath them. "I'd like that very much," she answered softly, "but I'll soon be returning to Dayton."

"Do you have to go?" Thad pleaded. He reached for her hand and the canoe wobbled.

Annabelle pulled away and clung to the canoe, but quickly recovered when she realized there was no threat of capsizing. The mood ruined, she complained, "Things aren't that easy, Thad. Right now I'm angry at Mattie."

"What's wrong? What did she do?"

Annabelle slowly spilled out the tragic tale—from her one-sided version, including a few details about Charles Harrison—and finishing with a bitter declaration, "I shall not forgive her!"

Thaddeas responded sympathetically, "What a shock. I can imagine how this upsets you."

"Oh, I knew you would understand, Thad."

As he paddled, he spoke, "It reminds me of another story I heard." Annabelle gazed at him skeptically.

"Yes, it's much like your situation. No," he argued with himself, "it's similar but different."

He succeeded to arouse her curiosity. "Really? How?"

"You want to hear it?" She nodded. "There were two women. Each bore a child out of wedlock, but one child died." Annabelle frowned and he asked, "Follow me?"

She nodded, and he continued, "The women fought over the living child."

"That's absurd."

"I agree, but at any rate, their dispute went before the king."

"This isn't a true story," Annabelle accused.

"Oh, but it is. Do you know what the king said?"

"No."

"Bring me a sword and I'll divide the living child in half and give one half to each woman."

"How awful. That can't be true," Annabelle insisted.

"Yes, it is. Then the real mother denied the child and said 'Give it to the other woman.'"

Annabelle puzzled over the story until Thad spoke again.

"The story is found in the Bible. You can look it up in I Kings chapter three. Do you understand?"

"I think so. The real mother loved the child enough to give it away." Silence hung for a full count. "Like Lacy's parents."

Thad had beached the canoe alongside a fallen tree where they had a good view of a beaver community. As they watched the creatures, he waited for Annabelle to digest his story. "Like Mattie," she mumbled. "I have to forgive her, don't I?"

"If you want to please Jesus, you have no other choice."

"Do you think He can give me peace about this?"

Thaddeas placed his hand alongside her troubled face and prayed in a soft tone, "Lord Jesus, please give Annabelle your peace. Help her to forgive Mattie, and heal their relationship. Amen."

Annabelle dabbed at puffy eyes. "Thaddeas, thank you so much. I must get this settled right away. Would you mind terribly if . . ."

"If we left?" he finished her statement. "No."

"Oh, Thad, you're wonderful."

"You think so?"

She nodded while he headed the canoe in the direction of Tucker House.

❧

Annabelle approached the closed bedroom door and stopped to listen. Hearing the heart-wrenching sobs of her aunt penetrate the walls, she pushed, and the door creaked open. Annabelle tried to focus in the darkness that engulfed the room.

"Mattie," she whispered.

The sobs ceased, then sounded intermittently, but she was summoned. "Come here, child."

She rushed to the spot where the voice had pierced the blackness and saw Mattie's shadow upon the mattress. "I'm sorry, Mattie. I forgive you. Of course, I do."

"Thank you, Jesus," Mattie exclaimed. "I don't deserve it.

I've done sech a great wrong."

"I understand now. You love us, that's all that matters."

"I love you so much, you'll never know."

"I think I do."

"I've carried this burden for so long," Mattie sighed.

"Does Buck know?"

"Yes."

Annabelle reached across the inky thickness and found Mattie's hand. "We need to tell Kate and Claire."

"Yes. Tomorrow." The sad tone of Mattie's voice softened Annabelle's heart.

"We'll do it together. Mattie?"

"Yes?"

"Maybe sometime you can tell me what my mother was like."

"I'd be proud to."

thirty

Kate lifted the calico curtain to peek out the window. She wondered, *Who could be riding up at this early hour?* A circle of dust accompanied the wagon containing Buck, Mattie, Annabelle, and Claire.

"Looks like we got company, boys." Little Gabe's eyes lit up.

"Who, Mama?" Wetness appeared in the corners of her eyes, for it was the first time Gabe had called her mama.

"Why, it's the Larsons, honey."

"Miss Annabelle and Miss Claire?" Little Gabe clapped chubby hands and ran toward the door, with his little brother close at heel.

"What a pretty picture this makes," Annabelle exclaimed, gathering Gabe into her arms as Claire scooped up Cody.

"Come on in." The tension in the air struck Kate at once.

Buck spoke up. "We come as a family to share some important news." The look on his face and the others' was so sober that Kate almost shuddered.

Ben entered the house at that moment, and Kate motioned him to her side, bringing him up-to-date. "Well, let's go into the sitting room. There are some toys there for the boys, and we can talk."

As the others seated themselves, Kate diverted Cody and Gabe's attention with the wooden horses and toy wagons that Ben had carved, and they soon were in their own little world of make-believe. "There now, what is it?"

Buck started, "Mattie and I have harbored some secrets that we should have shared with you girls years ago. Last night Annabelle learned the truth, and now Mattie wants to tell you her story, some facts about her past."

Mattie looked at Kate first. "We talked about some of this once, Kate. But Claire, you were too young at the time, so I'll start from the beginning.

"I made some mistakes when I was about your age. I met a man, named Lieutenant Wade Brooks, and had his child outa wedlock."

She paused and Kate interrupted. "But it wasn't your fault, Mattie." Claire's eyes grew big as pumpkins, amazed with this information and the fact that Kate and Annabelle both knew.

"I made wrong choices. It's always wrong not ta wait till you're married to be intimate with a man. My pa, a preacher, called me a harlot, threw me outa the house. The young man disappeared out of my life."

Mattie was amazed how much easier it was to tell the story this time. A calm possessed her. "'Twasn't his fault. We were both young and foolish. We lost track of each other. I went to my married sister, Elizabeth, and she took my baby to raise. That baby was you, Kate."

Mattie stopped, letting the words soak in. Kate cried, "Oh, Lord." Claire's shoulders shook as emotion overtook her.

"I made a new life for myself. Elizabeth bore two daughters, Annabelle and Claire. After the Indian raid that killed your folks, Claire, I came to get you all. I should have told you girls who I was." She looked at Claire, "Your aunt," then at Kate, "and your ma."

The room hung silent, except for the low noises the boys made in their play, until she went on. "I fell in love with Buck, but put him off for too many years because I didn't feel worthy of him."

He reached out to take her hand. "I shared my story with him, but I carried this burden too long. I release it to ya now. I pray you will forgive me, but won't hold it against ya if ya don't."

Kate and Claire immediately went to the broken woman. Claire spoke first, "Of course we forgive you, Mattie."

She looked at Kate. "Yes, I forgive you." Kate paused and then used the precious word, "Mother."

"I've given this a lot of thought," Annabelle interrupted, "and this does not really change a thing. You're still my sisters, as I see it." Everyone hugged and talked at once.

The boys giggled and jumped onto laps. "Me too, me too," said Cody, wanting to get in on the hugs and kisses. Wet smacks were planted on their cherub cheeks.

The rest of the facts were pieced together as they discussed this new disclosure. Annabelle explained to Ben that the prowler was Charles Harrison, whom the lieutenant had sent to spy out the truth.

Mattie assured Kate that the lieutenant had turned into an honorable man that she could respect. "He wants ta meet you, Kate, more than anythin' else in the world. You look like him, you have his eyes and dark hair. He said he has a son, fourteen years old. He'd be a half-brother to ya. Here, I wrote down Lieutenant Brook's address at Fort Wayne where he is stationed. I 'spect, if he'd get a letter from you he'd be down here in a flash." Kate nodded. Adrenalin pumped through her veins.

"Thank you, Mattie. This means so much to me. You have given me a f-father." She choked on the words and Ben placed his arm around her protectively.

Mattie stood and spoke to Kate. "You told me once that love is pain. I know that ta be a fact. I thank everyone of you in this room for forgivin' me. I'm so glad we all know the Lord, for I know 'tis Him that makes it possible."

Ben then gathered them together in a family circle, placing the boys and their toys in the middle by their feet. They joined hands and prayed.

❧

That evening back at Tucker House in the last hour of light,

Luke took Annabelle and Claire for a walk. The evening air invigorated them. "I think I'm getting soft and lazy," Luke admitted.

"Perhaps we need a run," Claire suggested.

"Race you to the creek," Annabelle shouted.

Luke never liked to lose, especially to women. He easily caught up to them and passed them like a storm on wheels.

He flung himself on the grassy embankment and crossed his legs, trying to control his panting. The girls arrived neck and neck and collapsed at his feet. "What took you so long?" he asked.

They both socked him playfully, as they sought to catch their breath.

"Look, the water was high here too." Claire pointed to the water line mark on the bank and referred to Dayton's floods. The thought sobered them, and they watched the mosquitoes hover over the water as they reflected.

Annabelle swatted at one that dined on her neck. "Ouch!"

"Better head back," Luke suggested. He helped them to their feet and commented. "This has been quite a visit. I'm real proud of both my girls." He now had one on each arm. He referred to Mattie's confession when he said, "You could have been bitter, but you've chosen forgiveness."

Claire answered, "All things are possible with Christ."

"Love is a miracle," Luke answered while looking intently at Annabelle. Then he seemed embarrassed and changed the subject. "We should be heading back for Dayton soon. How does the day after tomorrow sound?"

"Great!" Claire answered, who looked forward to returning to the orphanage.

"I won't be going back," Annabelle announced with resignation in her voice.

Claire understood, her heart aching for Luke. She tactfully excused herself. "I-I'll leave you two alone to talk about this."

They stood in silence until she was out of sight, pausing under the hickory tree. Luke turned toward her then to hear her explanation.

"I have to stay. I'm in love with Thaddeas." She saw the hurt expression on his face. "I'm sorry, Luke. I admire you, nearly worship you, but I cannot let myself grow to love you when I already love Thad. If I go back, I'll become even more fond of you, and it will hurt us."

He took her hands in both of his and looked at her with a steady gaze. As he did so, they were unaware of another presence nearby. Thaddeas, coming in search of them, rounded the corner of the house to catch this intimate moment. He stopped to watch from a distance, which made it impossible to hear what they were saying.

"I understand, Annabelle. I am growing very fond of you." He touched her chin with his finger. "May the Lord continue to bless you. Good-bye Annabelle." He pulled her into his arms and gave her a brotherly hug.

Thad took a few steps toward them and shouted angrily, "I see how it is then!" They jumped apart in shock, and watched him stomp off.

"Thaddeas, wait!" Annabelle ran after him while Luke ran his fingers through his sandy hair.

Thaddeas mounted his horse and kicked. The animal bolted, unused to this kind of touch from his master. The rider did not look back as his name was called. "Thaddeas!"

thirty-one

Annabelle embraced Claire. "I love you."

"I'll miss you," Claire said with much emotion.

"We've become so close." Annabelle held her sister at arm's length. "You've taught me so much. Thank you for convincing me to try Dayton last winter. I hope you understand why I have to stay."

Claire nodded. "I do. And don't worry." She squeezed Annabelle's arms. "It'll all work out fine. Just remember to keep praying."

"I will."

"Good-bye."

Annabelle nodded and released her sister. Then she turned to Luke while Mattie and Buck lavished Claire with farewells.

Stiffly, they faced each other. Luke spoke first, "I'm sorry Thaddeas misunderstood. Are you sure you don't want to come along and provoke him further?" he teased.

"I'm sure," Annabelle smiled.

"All right." Luke grinned. "Keep an eye on Cody and Gabe."

"I will." Annabelle almost wished she could return to the orphanage. It was hard to let Luke and Claire go. "You'll send my chest of belongings then?"

"I'll take care of it personally. Good-bye, Annabelle." Luke pulled her into a final embrace and then let her go.

❧

That afternoon, the heat bore down on Annabelle's back as she rode into Beaver Creek, rehearsing her speech. She reined Dusty in at the sheriff's office and her boots clacked on the wooden planks of the porch announcing her arrival—if someone had been in the office to hear it—but the sheriff was at Tucker House. It was Saturday, so Thad had the day off at the mill and was inside, sulking in his room.

Annabelle entered the empty office and her voice echoed as she called out. "Anybody here?"

When there was no answer, she turned to face the door that stood between her and her future, for she figured Thaddeas was on the other side. Swallowing for courage, Annabelle tapped lightly. A few seconds passed, then it opened slowly.

"Annabelle! You shouldn't be here." The words were spoken hotly.

"I probably shouldn't." She returned his glare. "A woman alone in a man's room . . . but I have to make you listen."

"Why don't you send me a telegram?"

Annabelle's cheeks burned at the insinuation, but she had to make him understand. "It wasn't what you thought last night with Luke."

"It's none of my business."

Annabelle sighed, "Thaddeas, please. There's nothing between Luke and me."

Thaddeas scowled.

"I was just telling him good-bye. I won't be going back to Dayton."

He stared at her, longing to believe. She returned his stare, then threw her arms in the air, surrendering. "Fine!" She turned to leave.

"Wait. Please, come in."

Annabelle settled down, picked up her skirt, and stepped over the threshold. The room, bare and masculine, was sparsely furnished. Her eyes fell upon the cot where he slept, covers in disarray.

Thaddeas took control of the situation. "Over here. Let's sit down." He directed her toward a small table with two chairs in the opposite corner of the room. Clumsily, he pulled one out for her, and she seated herself directly across from him.

"Now, what were you saying?" He wanted to get this straight, plain and simple.

She cleared her throat. "What you saw was not as it appeared. Of course, Luke and I are close friends, working together as we have. I hated to tell him that I would not be returning. He was just telling me in his own way that it was all right, and saying good-bye."

"I'm sorry, Annabelle. I'm glad you came." There was a pause, and their expressions softened.

"But you're right, I shouldn't be here," Annabelle said as she squirmed in her seat.

"Never mind that. Please stay. Tell me how things are going with you and Mattie."

"We got things worked out."

"I'm so glad. I knew you would."

Annabelle fumbled with her gloves. "We told Kate and Claire."

"How did they take it?"

"Better than I did. Everything is going to be all right." Thaddeas waited for her to finish. "Actually, nothing has really changed, except Kate has a new father and a brother."

Thaddeas listened. "Mattie said she's sending a letter to her own pa. He's been trying to get in touch with her, and she's finally forgiven him. Said when I forgave her, then she realized she had to forgive her folks for what they did to her."

"Annabelle, that's wonderful." Thaddeas reached across the table to take her hand. "You allowed the Lord to work through you, and it changed her heart. I'm so happy."

"Are you?"

"With you here, yes."

"When are you going to tell me what happened to Mary Beth?"

Thaddeas grinned. "She grew frustrated with me."

"Why is that?"

"I was pining away for you."

Annabelle reddened. "Then you were jealous the other night?"

"Terribly."

"I was miserable when you left that way," Annabelle confessed.

"I was too."

"I have just one more thing to say then."

"What is that?"

"Thaddeas Larson, if you don't marry me, I shall die!"

Thaddeas laughed, "I'm glad to see you didn't lose your spunk. Come here, Darling; of course I'll marry you."

He held out his arms and she flew into them, and he pulled her onto his lap, enveloping her. "I love you, Annabelle," he whispered against her ear.

"I love you, Thad."

He kissed her. "Will you be my wife?"

"Of course."

"What about your ambitions?"

Annabelle's face glowed. "Once I had lofty ambitions, now they are even loftier."

"So tell me, what are they?"

"To marry you and serve the Lord Jesus. What else would they be?"

"I cannot imagine any other thing."

A Letter To Our Readers

Dear Reader:

In order that we might better contribute to your reading enjoyment, we would appreciate your taking a few minutes to respond to the following questions. When completed, please return to the following:

Rebecca Germany, Editor
Heartsong Presents
P.O. Box 719
Uhrichsville, Ohio 44683

1. Did you enjoy reading *Lofty Ambitions*?
   ❑ Very much. I would like to see more books
      by this author!
   ❑ Moderately
      I would have enjoyed it more if _____

   _____

2. Are you a member of *Heartsong Presents*? Yes   No
   If no, where did you purchase this book? _____

   _____

3. What influenced your decision to purchase this
   book? (Check those that apply.)

   ❑ Cover   ❑ Back cover copy

   ❑ Title   ❑ Friends

   ❑ Publicity   ❑ Other _____

4. On a scale from 1 (poor) to 10 (superior), please rate
   the following elements.

   ___Heroine   ___Plot

   ___Hero   ___Inspirational theme

   ___Setting   ___Secondary characters

5. What settings would you like to see covered in
   Heartsong Presents books?

   _____

   _____

6. What are some inspirational themes you would like
   to see treated in future books?_____

   _____

   _____

7. Would you be interested in reading other *Heartsong
   Presents* titles?   ❏ Yes   ❏ No

8. Please check your age range:
   ❏ Under 18   ❏ 18-24   ❏ 25-34
   ❏ 35-45   ❏ 46-55   ❏ Over 55

9. How many hours per week do you read? _____

Name _____

Occupation _____

Address _____

City _____ State _____ Zip _____

Norene Morris

Historical Trilogy

___*Cottonwood Dreams*—The pioneer town of Venture, Kansas was all Mary Lou had ever known. One day changed everything. Mary Lou longed to be a rancher's wife. Was it time to give up her dream? HP12 $2.95

___*Rainbow Harvest*—Newly married Mary Lou and Tom leave her frontier home in Kansas for Tom's ranch in Texas. Mary Lou and Tom have seen God work miracles in their own lives. Now they are praying that God will bring a similar harvest in the lives of those they love. HP39 $2.95

___*Pioneer Legacy*—Traveling from Texas to Kansas in the late 1800s, Mary Lou and Tom Langdon, along with their twins, have many trying experiences. As her old home looms nearer, Mary Lou wonders how she and her family will be received. HP107 $2.95

···· Hearts ♥ ng ····

·········· Presents ·

Great Inspirational Romance at a Great Price!

Heartsong Presents books are inspirational romances in contemporary and historical settings, designed to give you an enjoyable, spirit-lifting reading experience. You can choose from 108 wonderfully written titles from some of today's best authors like Colleen L. Reece, Brenda Bancroft, Janelle Jamison, and many others.

When ordering quantities less than twelve, above titles are $2.95 each.

BESTSELLERS
from

BALLANTINE BOOKS

RABBIT BOSS, Thomas Sanchez	$1.95
THE SENSUOUS COUPLE, Robert Chartham	$1.50
WHAT TURNS WOMEN ON, Robert Chartham	$1.50
THE SECRET TEAM: THE CIA AND ITS ALLIES, L. Fletcher Prouty	$1.95
THE ANDERSON PAPERS, Jack Anderson	$1.75
SWEET STREET, Jack Olsen	$1.50
THE TEACHINGS OF DON JUAN, Carlos Castaneda	$1.25
ENEMY AT THE GATES, William Craig	$1.95
SUPER MARRIAGE-SUPER SEX, H. Freedman	$1.50
REVOLUTIONARY SUICIDE, Huey Newton	$1.95
LONG SUMMER DAY, R. F. Delderfield	$1.50
BACK TO THE TOP OF THE WORLD, Hans Ruesch	$1.50
THE IPCRESS FILE, Len Deighton	$1.50
CITY POLICE, Jonathan Rubinstein	$1.95
POST OF HONOR, R. F. Delderfield	$1.50
THE UFO EXPERIENCE, J. Allen Hynek	$1.50

At your local bookstore, or

To order by mail, send price of book(s) plus 25¢ per order for handling to Ballantine Cash Sales, P.O. Box 505, Westminster, Maryland 21157. Please allow three weeks for delivery.

And suddenly Duddy did smile. He laughed. He grabbed Max, hugged him, and spun him around. "You see," he said, his voice filled with marvel. "You see."